House on Waterfall Hill

HOLLY MARTIN

CHAPTER ONE

Flick negotiated her little purple Mini through the twisty country lanes as she made her way to Lovegrove Bay at the furthest end of Cornwall.

What was she doing?

Her nan had emotionally blackmailed her into taking over Waterfall House just a few weeks ago and, with Flick's childhood ties to the seaside town and with her being currently jobless and soon to be homeless, Flick had agreed but now she was having doubts. Well, she'd had doubts from the start.

She had six months to turn around the finances of Waterfall House, a large Victorian style building filled with rooms selling different crafts from local artists, otherwise when her nan got back from her six months in Australia she was going to sell the whole thing to a hotel developer. It was in a prime position on the clifftops overlooking the sleepy little seaside town of

Lovegrove Bay and her nan had been approached many times to sell the place.

But Flick didn't have the first idea how to run a business. Sadly neither did her nan which was why she barely had a penny to her name and Waterfall House hadn't sold a single item since Christmas. Her nan hadn't even had enough to fly out to Australia to help look after her sister after surgery, her sister had to pay for that.

The trouble was the house didn't even have a café anymore, which had been very successful back in the day. Her nan had stopped doing that side of things years before when her chef quit and she couldn't get anyone to replace him. So sadly the art studios didn't even have that revenue or footfall to fall back on anymore – the kind of people who would stop by for a sandwich and then also buy a few knick-knacks. The other problem was the things on sale weren't actually cheap knick-knacks but wooden sculptures that cost seven hundred pounds or paintings that cost three thousand pounds. Lovegrove Bay had a large retiree population and in the summer months the town was filled with average families, the types of people who would spend money on crazy golf or the amusements on the pier, but not the types of people who would spend three thousand pounds on a painting.

Somehow Flick had to get more people to visit the house on Waterfall Hill and either they had to be the kinds of people who had hundreds to spend on a beautifully embroidered quilt, or she'd have to get the artists to create more accessible artwork – and she knew that wasn't going to go down well.

Maybe she could get Luke Donnelly on her side. He was going to be her flatmate. The top floor of the Victorian town house had been converted into a two-bedroom flat and her nan had spent the last six months living with a man who was a third of her age. It seemed like an unlikely friendship but somehow it had worked.

Flick reached the top of the hill and could see the whole of Lovegrove Bay laid out below her, twinkling in the moonlight. All the houses, seemingly piled on top of each other, looked cute with their windows lit up with golden lights. She had spent every school holiday here with her nan and grandad, playing on the beach, sitting on the harbour wall eating an ice cream, or fish and chips, spending her pennies on the arcades on the pier. She had loved it here but it had been many years since she'd come back. Life had just got in the way.

She rounded the corner and there was Waterfall House or, as the locals knew it, the House with the Wonky Tree.

The tree itself was a giant sycamore tree that gave the Leaning Tower of Pisa a run for its money. It was such an unusual-shaped landmark, bent over as if in a gale force wind, that it often ended up on thousands of Instagram photos. Over the years, it had been fortified with various cables and poles to stop it falling over completely because cutting it down was unthinkable. It was looking a little worse for wear though now; it was the middle of summer and it should be full of leaves but only half the branches had a handful of leaves on. Her nan had called an arborist for it the year before and he'd said that because the tree was growing at such an angle the roots were coming away from the soil and it wasn't getting the nutrients it needed. Unfortunately, there wasn't a lot they could do to save it. Thankfully if it did ever give up the ghost and fall, it was leaning in such a way that it would land in the private garden next to the house and miss the house completely. Flick had spent many an hour climbing it, hanging from it, sitting underneath it, even drawing it. It was as much part of her childhood memories as the house itself.

She turned her attention to the house. Waterfall House was a large four-storey house with little nooks, unusual-shaped rooms and little stairs that curled up to tucked-away secret places. It even had two turrets. It had been the perfect place to play for a little girl with a big imagination.

Waterfall House had been here as far back as Flick could remember and she'd loved watching the artists creating their masterpieces. It had inspired a love of being creative in her. She spent a lot of time painting or making crafty things. She wasn't particularly good at it but she always enjoyed it.

Her grandad had bought the house before Flick was born and after many months of renovations, he'd opened it as an artists' retreat. He'd had a stroke a few years before that, which he'd talked about often as being the thing that saved him. He'd been in a high-powered job in London which was always fast-paced and very stressful and he said that it was only a matter of time before he burned himself out completely, had some kind of nervous breakdown or died of a heart attack. The stroke had been a huge wake-up call and he'd changed his life completely, taking early retirement and relocating to Lovegrove Bay. He'd talked often about his rehabilitation after the stroke and how much art therapy had helped him. Once he was back on his feet, he'd decided he'd wanted to open a place where he could run art workshops to help others with brain injuries and that was how the idea for Waterfall House came about. Later the workshops were extended to encompass anyone who had suffered any kind of physical injury that needed physiotherapy or some kind of rehabilitation. Hundreds of people had come through the doors over the years and aided their recovery with painting, clay work or other arts and crafts. Over the years it had developed into a space where artists could sell their work too. Sadly after her granddad had died, the workshops had dried up; her nan hadn't wanted to run them in his place or get someone in to replace him, so it had just become this space where artists made and sold their work instead. But now even that was failing.

Flick pulled up outside and got out and looked around. Even in the darkness she could see how tired the place looked. It had always had pale pink walls but a lot of the paint was peeling away, as it was on the wooden window frames. Her grandad had painstakingly laid some hexagonal stepping stones that led to the front door, but some of these were cracked, missing or half buried under dirt. It desperately needed some TLC, although as there was no money to do so, they would have to make do with what they had for now.

She was too tired to think right now after her long drive from London and now she was faced with introducing herself to Luke, someone who, despite having lived with her nan for the last six months, she knew very little about. Her limited experience of artists at various craft shows was that they were a pompous bunch who looked down at her *pathetic* efforts. Although she wouldn't be sharing any of her art tonight, she didn't want to face anyone who behaved that way.

It was a shame her nan had left two weeks before, it would have been nice if she'd been there to introduce her to Luke and the other artists. It would have certainly made things easier.

She grabbed one of her bags, the rest could wait until morning. She let herself in with the key her nan had sent her and made her way up the back staircase to the top-floor flat. She hovered outside for a second wondering if she should knock but this was her home now, she shouldn't have to knock to go into her own home. But equally she didn't want to just walk in on him. He could be doing anything.

She knocked but there was no sound behind the

door, no call to say he was on his way to answer it, not even the sound of the TV. She knocked again but when there was still silence on the other side, she let herself in.

'Hello!' she called but there was no noise at all to indicate that someone was home.

She wasn't expecting a welcome home party but she'd kind of thought he'd be there. She'd told her nan what time she was arriving and assumed that information had been passed on. Was he not at least a bit curious about who he was going to be sharing a flat with for the next six months? Or was this some kind of silent protest against having a new boss foisted on him?

Although Flick was actually a little bit relieved he wasn't here. She was too tired to deal with any confrontation tonight.

The flat looked comfortable and clean. A large horseshoe-shaped sofa stood in the middle of the room, with an open-plan kitchen and dining area up one end and a few doors leading off the main living area.

She looked around trying to find out more information about the man she was going to be living with. He was clean and tidy, that was something. A bookshelf was filled with books which had to be his. Her nan was a big romance reader and these books with their mostly black covers were definitely not romance. She wandered closer. You could tell a lot about a person from their bookcase. She could see all of Tolkien's books, *The Lord of the Rings* and *The Hobbit* obviously but some of his lesser-known titles too like *The Adventures of Tom Bombadil* and *The Silmarillion*. She loved *The Lord of the Rings* though she secretly loved the film more than the books, although she would never admit that to any of the die-hard Tolkien fans. Luke had some of her favourite Terry Pratchett books too, plus *Game of Thrones* and *The Wheel of Time*. He clearly loved his fantasy, which was a bonus for her. Although she would read pretty much any genre, fantasy was probably her favourite. There were also some well-thumbed copies of Shakespeare's plays as well as more classical literature like Dickens's *Oliver Twist* and Mary Shelley's *Frankenstein*, and a whole range of Agatha Christie. She liked that he had diverse tastes.

She wondered which room was hers. All the doors were closed. She'd only been a child when she'd last been up here, and back then it had been used just as guest bedrooms for people attending the retreats The last time she had visited her nan, she'd still been living in a tiny cottage in the main part of the village before her nan had sold that to help to fund this place.

She approached the first door, knocked and, when there was no sound from within, she opened it and saw a large bathroom which was all white but with seaside paraphernalia everywhere. She moved to the door next to it and knocked again. There was still silence on the other side so she opened it and froze.

This was definitely not her room, she could tell that from the man standing naked on the other side. She noticed he had earphones in his ears, which was probably the reason he hadn't heard her, but she couldn't help noticing that he seemed to be studying himself in the mirror and one area of his body seemed to be holding his attention, avidly.

She screamed in shock. His eyes widened in horror as he saw her and he screamed too, grabbing a cushion to hide his manhood. She quickly hurried from the room but she heard him chase after her.

'I'm so sorry, I knocked but there was no answer.' Flick cringed. Of all the ways to introduce herself to her new flatmate, this had to be the worst.

'Flick wait, I can explain.'

'No need.' Flick waved her hand, hurrying to the door on the other side of the room. 'What you do in the privacy of your own bedroom is none of my business.'

'Flick, please.'

She stopped to look at him, cautiously, and thankfully his manhood was hidden behind a cushion.

'I'm so sorry,' the man, presumably Luke, said.

'What do you have to be sorry about, I barged in on you,' Flick said, shaking her head. So much for first impressions.

'I'm sorry for the way we met,' he gestured back to his room. 'I wasn't expecting you this early, I thought I'd have a shower so I was somewhat presentable and I hadn't realised you were here.' He looked at his watch. 'Oh, you're not early at all. I must have lost track of time. Look… I'm not a vain person, I don't spend hours looking at myself in the mirror, styling my hair. I barely glance at myself before I go out, just enough to check that the t-shirt or jumper I'm wearing isn't too stained. And I'm not ridiculously proud of my… tackle that I like to stare at it in the mirror. I…' he sighed heavily. 'My dad died of testicular cancer when he was thirty-one, the same age I am now, and it's just made me super paranoid about it. I check myself for lumps every week, I know that sounds weird but—'

'It's not weird, I check my breasts regularly too.'

'That's… important to do.'

'It is.'

They stared at each other. They had strayed into very weird territory with this conversation. They hadn't even been properly introduced yet, and they were talking to each other about examining their bodies as easily as if they were talking about a favourite pizza topping. Would now be a good time to introduce herself? Although Flick didn't exactly think it was appropriate to hold out a hand for him to shake as he was standing there with only a cushion to protect his modesty.

He had a nice body. It was strong, muscular and toned but not defined by hours down the gym; his muscles, large arms and thighs looked more natural than they would if they'd been achieved by lifting weights. He had a lovely face too, behind those black-rimmed glasses he was wearing.

Jesus Christ, why was she checking him out? And he must have seen her do it too, her eyes roaming all over his body. Now really wasn't the time.

She gestured to the door behind her.

'I'm going to go to my room and when I see you next we'll just pretend this whole debacle never happened.'

'I like the sound of that.'

She moved over to the door and tentatively pushed that open. It was decorated in pale blue but there was nothing in here to suggest this was where her nan normally slept. In fact there was nothing in the rest of the flat that looked like her nan lived there either. Maybe she had cleared the bedroom out for Flick or maybe her nan was a lot more minimalist than she'd remembered.

She looked back into the lounge to find that Luke was still watching her.

'I'm not being creepy, I just don't want to show you my bum as I go back to my room.'

She smirked and gave him a wave before closing the bedroom door.

The bed looked so inviting and, despite it being only nine o'clock, she was exhausted from driving so she decided to call it a night and hope that by the morning she could introduce herself to her new flatmate properly.

She changed into her sleep shorts and vest and climbed into bed. She stared at the ceiling, trying to shake the image of a naked Luke Donnelly from her mind, recognising that spark of attraction as it bloomed to life in her chest. She shook her head, she didn't need complications. She was here to save the art studios and things could get messy if she got involved with one of the artists and her flatmate. She knew her best friend,

Tabitha, would say something complicated and messy was exactly what Flick needed, that she should let her hair down and have some fun. But she would keep things friendly but professional between her and Luke. Feeling better after making that decision she rolled over and within a few minutes she'd drifted off to sleep.

CHAPTER TWO

Flick woke early hours in the morning while it was still dark. The weather had been so hot lately that even the night times didn't provide any respite. She opened the window and then walked out into the kitchen to get a drink. The main living area was in darkness but moonlight was pouring through the large windows that overlooked the bay. She got herself a glass of water and then went to stand in front of the window to admire the view. The sea was mirror-calm, the cliffs, houses and the moon reflecting off the water perfectly.

Just then Luke's bedroom door opened and he came out but stopped when he saw her.

She didn't know what to say to him, it was still awkward between them. She'd seen him naked and, despite him saying he wasn't proud of his tackle, he certainly didn't have anything to be shy about. She rubbed her eyes, trying to scrub that image from her mind. They were supposed to pretend that had never happened but she wasn't sure how she'd do that.

He stuck out a hand. 'Hello, I'm Luke Donnelly.'

She smiled and shook his hand. 'Flick Hunter.'

'Good to meet you, Flick. I was just going to grab something to eat, did you… did you want to join me?'

'I didn't bring any food with me but I can contribute towards your food until I get a chance to go shopping for myself.'

He stared at her in confusion. 'Your nan didn't tell you anything about me, did she?'

That was a weird response. 'No, what do I need to know?'

He dismissed it with a wave of his hand. 'It doesn't matter. But actually me and your nan always shared the grocery shop and we shared the cooking but we can sort that out later. For now, help yourself to any food in the house and you don't need to worry about paying me back.'

'Well, I'll make sure I replace whatever I use.'

'You really don't need to worry about that. I was only going to make myself some peanut butter on toast, would that suit you?'

Her stomach gurgled appreciatively.

'I'll take that as a yes,' Luke said.

He moved into the kitchen area and started making the food.

'Can I help?'

He shook his head. 'It won't take me a few minutes.'

She perched on a bar stool and studied him. His t-shirt was crumpled, his hair was dark and floppy like he just never really bothered to comb it, his jeans had holes in and, although she knew that you could pay thousands of pounds for distressed-look designer jeans just like those, she knew somehow the holes were from years of wear not some cool designer look. He was also wearing odd socks, one green, one blue. But there was something cute and adorable about him, like an oversized puppy. He was a good-looking man, with warm brown eyes and a nice smile. He was large too, easily six foot, and with arms that were strong without being too muscly. She could see there would be many a woman who would want to fix him up. Not her though, her life was a mess as it was, she wasn't in any position to fix other people. Besides, Luke shouldn't change who he was for any woman. She was strongly of the belief that people should love you for who you are, not try to make you into something you're not.

She smiled at his t-shirt which had a picture of a cave troll on it from *Lord of the Rings*.

'I was admiring your book collection when I arrived,' Flick said, deliberately not mentioning that had been seconds before she had seen him naked – even now she was thinking about seeing him in all his glory again.

'Oh yeah, I'm a bit of a nerd when it comes to the books I read.'

'You're not a nerd, you have excellent taste. You have some of my favourite books over there. I love *Lord of the Rings*.'

He turned to look at her, his eyes narrowed as if he thought she was mocking him. 'Really?'

'Honestly, I've read it at least three times and not many books get a repeat viewing as there are always so many more out there I want to read. But that, *The Hobbit* and anything by Pratchett are my go-to favourites.'

'Oh god, will you marry me?'

She laughed. 'You might want to hold off on that proposal until you hear my sordid secret.'

'What's that?'

'I think the films are better.'

Luke clutched his heart as if it was suddenly broken. 'OK, wedding's off. Actually I love the films too, though I'm not sure if one is better than the other, just different.'

'That's a good attitude to take.'

He turned his attention back to the toast for a moment. 'What's your favourite Pratchett?'

'That's like asking which is your favourite child. What if the other books hear me?'

His smile was wide when he turned back to face her. 'Just whisper it, they haven't got very good hearing.'

She loved that he was playing along with her silliness. 'OK.' She lowered her voice. '*The Bromeliad Trilogy*.'

He nodded approvingly. 'Good choice.'

'It's just Pratchett at his very best. I think he was so much more comfortable writing for children than he was for adults. And who doesn't love a story about gnomes?'

'Well that's true.' He placed a plate down in front of

her with two slices of toast slathered in peanut butter and weirdly she'd watched him make a flask of tea.

'Shall we take these upstairs?'

'Upstairs?' She'd been to this house many times as a child, but this was the top floor. There was no upstairs.

'We finally got the roof terrace that your nan has always wanted.'

Flick gasped. 'Oh, she was always talking about that but she always had so many plans and projects that never happened or were never finished. And she's never exactly been flush for cash.'

'Well I, umm… I did it for her. She kept talking about it and we already had the flat roof up there so we just had to add the railings and the stairs, get it checked and approved by building regulations, it wasn't a big deal. And it benefits me too so it kind of made sense. Come on, I'll show you.'

Flick looked around; she hadn't seen any stairs when she came in.

Luke walked off to his room and returned a few moments later with two jumpers and a blanket. He passed a jumper to her and pulled one on himself.

'It gets a bit cool up there, even at this time of year.'

He grabbed his plate and the flask and walked towards the linen closet. She frowned in confusion but when she looked inside she saw a spiral staircase going up towards the roof.

'Stay here a sec, I just need to go up and open the roof hatch.'

She watched him climb up the stairs as she pulled on

his soft jumper that smelled wonderfully of him, spicy and fruity. He opened the hatch and then climbed out onto the roof, bending down and gesturing for her to come up.

She got to the top of the stairs and he held out a hand to help her onto the roof. She looked around. It was quite a large area that was in the shape of a raindrop, the pointy end jutting out towards the sea. It was surrounded by black wrought-iron railings and filled with potted plants and flowers that scented the air with a beautiful perfume. Little fairy lights were hung over the railings and twinkled around them. There was a sofa and a large round sun-lounger-type bed that could probably hold three or four people. But the view of the bay was the thing that held her attention. From up here it was completely unhindered, and she could see all the pretty coloured houses, the church tower overlooking the town, the long, white sandy beaches that even in the darkness seemed to glitter under the moonlight. She had always loved Lovegrove Bay, and that view was a reminder of so many happy memories here. This place was peaceful.

For the first time she wondered if this move could become permanent. She didn't have a job or a home to return to and her friends had moved from London one by one and, while she was still in touch with a few of them, she didn't see them very often anymore.

In fact the week before she'd come here she'd celebrated her thirtieth birthday alone. Her friends had all sent presents and cards and messages of course, but no one had been able to come down to see her. Flick understood, they all had young families and job commitments but it reinforced for her that she had nothing to go back to London for.

But could this be her new home? She'd have to get a job, once her nan came back and her work at the studio was finished. And she'd need a home, maybe a one-bedroom flat down in the main part of the town, and that wouldn't be easy knowing how much places went for round here. But maybe she could start over, make a life for herself here in Lovegrove Bay.

Luke watched her standing at the railings, her dark hair catching the light of the moon so it glittered like bronze as it moved in a gentle breeze, and thought she looked spectacular. It had been a long time since he'd been attracted to a woman, or rather since he'd allowed himself to be attracted to one. Falling in love only led to getting hurt. And since the whole town had found out who he was, he'd never been able to trust that the women who flirted with him were interested in him for him. So he'd squirrelled himself away up here, concentrated on his work and hadn't let silly things like relationships get in the way.

And along came Flick, who was pretty and kind and, more importantly, didn't know who he was, at least for now. And while it was very unlikely she would have any feelings for him, especially after their not so auspicious start, at least he knew their friendship right now and the way she treated him was genuine and not led by ulterior motives.

'This view is wonderful.'

'It really is.' He cleared his throat and focussed on the view in question instead. 'I spend every chance I get up here.'

'I can see why.' She moved to the point of the terrace. 'This is like a ship's stern.'

'I said the same. We've often joked about putting up a ship's sail or getting a big mermaid to sit there at the front.'

She laughed and stuck her arms out either side of her like she was flying and started singing Celine Dion's My Heart Will Go On.

He couldn't help but smile at her recreating the famous scene from *Titanic* when Rose and Jack are pretending to fly at the front of the ship. So he did what every self-respecting man would do faced with this situation. He moved behind her and stretched out his arms so he was flying too. She looked behind and laughed so hard at him joining her and that made him feel warm inside. She rolled her fingers over the top of his, entwining them with his just like Rose did to Jack in the movie, but stroking his fingers made his heart leap. It felt strangely intimate to be almost holding hands with this woman he barely knew.

She turned around laughing, her eyes alight with joy, and god damn it if she didn't steal a little bit of his heart in that moment. He was shocked by how much he suddenly wanted to cup her face and kiss her, but he'd never been one of those men who would seize the day. He was always the sort who would worry about the consequences of such an action and mostly how awkward it would be if she was horrified by it. And she probably would be horrified, they'd known each other for a few minutes so he was surprised by this sudden need to kiss her. This feeling, this pull to her didn't make any sense. He didn't know her. He wasn't the sort to believe you could fall for someone as soon as you'd met, he'd never believed in love at first sight and, while he was pretty sure this wasn't that, he had never wanted to kiss a woman so soon before. Maybe it was that they shared a common ground in books or that she made him smile so much. But whatever it was, knowing how inappropriate these unexpected feelings were, he took a step back instead, letting her move away from the railings.

'I love that film,' she said. 'I once went on a cruise and was so excited I'd get to recreate that moment, albeit on my own. I was so disappointed when I realised that part of the ship was closed off to the public. I wonder if they started doing that after too many people fell overboard recreating that *Titanic* moment.'

'Probably,' Luke said, moving over to the sofa and sitting down, hoping she hadn't noticed that he'd wanted to kiss her.

She sat down next to him on the sofa and tucked into her toast. He did the same, watching her as she looked out on the bay.

'It's so beautiful,' she said, softly.

'It is, I shall miss that view when I'm gone.'

She looked at him in surprise. 'You're leaving?'

He frowned. 'Yeah, did your nan not tell you?'

'No, I'm afraid I don't know anything about you other than you've lived with my nan for the last six months and that you're "a nice boy".'

Luke smiled. 'Is that what she said?'

'Yeah, she's very fond of you.'

Nice was a word a lot of women had said about him but never in favourable terms. *Too nice* was the most common description as if it was something bad. Although he didn't mind Audrey describing him in that way.

'Where are you going?' Flick asked.

'I'm moving to the Isle of Skye.'

'Oh that's a beautiful place, I've hiked around there, it's so pretty. They have a gorgeous little harbour village called Portree.'

'That's where I'm moving to, I have a house right on the water's edge. It has a massive studio out the back to do my work. It's a beautiful old house and I'm looking forward to doing it up, making it my own. And Skye is one of my favourite places. I'm going to get myself a dog and hike all over the island every day. It will be peaceful and remote and honestly I'm so excited.'

'What made you want to move all the way up there? It sounds like you're swapping one beachside house with a studio for another.'

He chewed his lip as he thought about how to

answer that question. In truth, since everyone in the town had found out who he was, life in Lovegrove Bay had become untenable. He wanted to walk the streets without people giving him funny looks or striking up a conversation with him purely because of what he could do for them. He'd always considered himself to be a kind and generous man but that generosity was starting to wear a little thin. But he couldn't tell Flick any of that, not yet anyway.

'There are… things that have happened recently that I'd like to get away from,' Luke said, cringing at how ambiguous and mysterious that sounded. She was bound to want to know more.

'Women,' Flick said, knowingly.

'Well, that's part of it,' Luke said, truthfully. There were lots of women around the town who he'd like to avoid lately. Some of them had made it their mission to get him to date them, making him retreat into his shell even more.

'Relationships are hard,' Flick said. 'And when they come to an end, sometimes it's only natural to run far away from them. I get that.'

He frowned. She thought he was running away from an ex. Oh well, that was easier than explaining the truth. 'I'm looking forward to making a fresh start,' he said, honestly.

'Funny, I was just thinking the same about coming here. I'm not sure there's anything for me in London anymore. And I love it here, it's one of my favourite places. And not to be rude or opportunistic but with you gone, maybe I could move in with my nan for a few months while I save up enough money to get my own place.'

'That doesn't sound rude at all,' Luke teased.

'It was a little. And so is my next question. When do you leave?'

He laughed. 'Three weeks. Well maybe four. I exchanged contracts yesterday actually and the official date I get the keys is just over a week from now. Although I'm having some work done on it before I move in, so it'll probably be four weeks until I actually go. Is that soon enough for you?'

She laughed. 'It's a shame actually. You know when you meet someone and you just know you're going to be very good friends? I get that feeling about you. There's not many people who would have reenacted the famous scene from *Titanic* with me. I think we could have been good together. We'd have had fun. Still, we can make the most of the time we have left.'

He looked at her because he got that feeling too, there was something about her he knew he could really connect with. If only he'd been staying long enough to find out.

'So what is it you do?' Flick asked.

He thought about whether to bypass the earlier part of his working life. He really didn't want her to know who he was, at least not yet, but he didn't want to lie to her either. 'Well, I used to make music for adverts or products, a ten or twenty-second music clip that would become synonymous with that brand. It wasn't something I particularly enjoyed, I fell into it somehow but it turned out I was quite good at making a catchy little ditty. But I've, erm... made some good decisions in my life which have meant I can concentrate on doing what I love, which is wood carving and sculpting.'

'Oh you're the wood carver, that's cool. Nan showed me some of the pieces that have gone on sale lately, you have an incredible talent.'

He smiled. 'Thank you. And what is it you do? Audrey said you're quite crafty yourself. Will you be opening up your own studio space?'

'Oh no, it's just fun stuff, it's not real art.'

'What is it?'

She looked embarrassed and he felt a bit bad for pushing her.

'Well, they're not in the same league as your work. You're an artist and I... I love what I do but it's not art. I make wish jars. I use real dandelions which I pick with the fluffy heads. The stems are hollow so I use craft wire up each one to keep it upright and then I stick it in a jar with some fairy lights and little handmade toadstools, leaves, berries, moss, so it looks like a little piece of an enchanted woodland inside the jar.'

She pulled her phone out of her pyjama pocket to show him some pictures of them and he couldn't help smiling at how cute they were. 'These are wonderful and I can see they'd be really popular.'

'You really like them?'

'Yes, they're sweet, whimsical, magical. Do you sell a lot of these? Is this your job?'

'They're popular when I do craft shows but no, I don't make a living from them. They're just something fun for me to make on evenings or weekends. No, employment-wise, I've had too many jobs to count, nothing particularly fun or fulfilling. I worked in a bank, a hotel, a plastics factory, sold double glazing, worked in a bingo hall. Nothing glamorous but it's paid the bills. I recently was made redundant from the marketing department of a company that sells and rents coffee vending machines.'

She looked at him as if expecting him to laugh at that but there wasn't anything funny about someone working hard for a living. He had got ridiculously lucky to be able to spend his days doing what he loved. He wondered if he could do that for her.

'What's the dream?'

'What do you mean?'

'Your dream job, what would you want to do more than anything?'

'Oh, that's not showy or glamorous either. Some people's dreams are big, life-changing dreams but mine are quite small really.'

'Go on.'

She finished her toast. 'I spent a lot of time here as a child and, as much as I adored Lovegrove Bay, it was this place that meant the most to me. Watching people create their masterpieces brought me so much joy. It motivated me to make my own art: paintings, clay, jewellery making. I was never very good at it but I enjoyed the process. I don't know if you know but my grandad started Waterfall House so he could teach therapeutic art workshops to help people with brain injuries. I found that so inspiring.'

Luke nodded. 'My mum was one of his students. She'd had a stroke too and she came over from Ireland to spend four weeks here doing one of his art workshops. It helped her so much, she came back a changed woman, she was so much happier and more confident.'

'Oh, I didn't realise.'

'Your grandad touched a lot of people.'

She smiled at that. 'So is that why you're here?'

'Yes, sort of. She came here for five different workshops, over a year or so. On the second one, she met a man called George and fell completely head over heels in love. She came home and signed up for a third workshop a few months later, which George was on as well. It was so good to see her smiling again, she had never been truly happy since my dad died. By the end of the fourth workshop she'd decided to move to England to be with George. She came home, sold the house and moved to Lovegrove Bay. Shortly after that she married him. I'd moved to London shortly before with work so when she moved here I visited her and my new stepfather often and I just fell in love with Lovegrove Bay. It's such a lovely, quiet, friendly community and the views are pretty spectacular. When she died, a few months after George, I still visited often. This place captured my mum's heart and imagination and almost all of her art was inspired by the town or the wonky tree. I think being here allowed me to feel closer to her. Eventually I made the move down here more permanent. And when the opportunity came up for me to be an artist here I leapt at it. I've been here four years now and moved in here six months ago.'

'I love that you're now living in the same place that brought your mum so much joy and inspiration.'

'Yeah, I do too. I will be sorry to leave it in many ways. But sorry, you were telling me about your dream job.'

'Oh yes, well the art therapy is linked to that in a way. I never really understood the importance of art in physical recovery until I was older, although I could see how much the clients enjoyed it. A friend of mine, Tabitha, had serious brain trauma in a car accident and she says building things with Lego or making things with clay was basically her saviour during her recovery. She did a ton of research into it, I think that side of things helped her cope too. And I did too so I could find out the best way to help her. Art can help with manual dexterity and fine motor skills which are so important after an accident. But it also helps with neuroplasticity, which is the brain's incredible ability to rewire itself where there is damage. After an accident, some people lose the ability to dress themselves or walk or talk or feed themselves because the part of their brain that takes care of those jobs has been damaged. Neuroplasticity means the brain can find another path around the damage to be able to do normal things like talk and walk or hold a mug of tea. And being creative can help unlock that. It's also important for people's mental health, to boost their confidence and help to express their emotions. That's why something as simple as adult colouring books were so popular a few years ago. We need that creative outlet.'

She picked up a crumb and popped it in her mouth. 'When I was little I wanted others to have that joy I'd seen from the artists here too, that feel-good feeling of making something. I used my pocket money to buy craft things like ribbons, buttons, quilling paper, paints, small canvases and sold them to my classmates at a small profit. When I was older I did the same sort of thing at craft fairs. I'd have a stand selling all the things you'd need to do different crafts, I'd sell kits for embroidery including the pattern and all the embroidery threads and buttons you'd need to complete it, mosaic kits, sock animal kits, plus lots of other crafty paraphernalia. But although the stall and kits were very popular, mostly I would only just about break even after paying for my table at the craft fair, so I gave up. But that's the dream, that one day I'll have my own shop selling craft paraphernalia to help spread that joy.'

An idea started bubbling in Luke's mind. 'You could do that here.'

'I don't think I know the first thing about running a business, not sure why my nan trusted me with saving the place. I have no idea what I'm going to do. There obviously needs to be some big changes.'

He frowned. 'What do you mean? Why does it need to change?'

She stared at him in surprise. 'Because it's not

making any money. Nan said there hasn't been a single sale since Christmas. For anyone.'

'Oh crap, I didn't realise.'

'She hasn't spoken to you about this?'

'No.'

'But you must have noticed that you haven't sold anything?'

'I sell a lot of my sculptures online and I get commissions, so honestly I hadn't really paid any attention to the fact that none of those sales had come from here.'

'What about the others? Have you spoken to them?'

'Well yes, but not normally about finances or sales, or rather the lack of them. And some of them have their own Etsy stores or websites so I presume they're making sales elsewhere too. Well I hope they are.'

'Maybe this place just isn't needed anymore. Maybe that's the trouble, more and more people are buying things online and places like this just get forgotten.'

'Well, maybe we need to remind people that we're still here.'

'Yeah, I'm just not sure how.'

He sighed. 'You're right about the online thing, you could probably go on Amazon and buy a Monet replica for a tenner. No one cares about real craftsmanship anymore or the hard work that goes into producing a unique work of art. Take that pirate, for example,' Luke said, gesturing to a sculpture of a pirate's face on the back wall made entirely of different chains and tools. 'It took Derek two weeks to do that. He used to have a studio here but he moved to the town a few years ago.'

'It's wonderful. I love the detail. But I think you're wrong. You invite people from the town up here and most of them would love the embroidered quilts or paintings – most people can totally appreciate the amount of work that goes into one of your sculptures – but the average family or couple couldn't afford it no matter how much they love it. A lot of people are having to make the choice between buying food or paying bills and buying a three-thousand-pound wooden sculpture or a thousand-pound painting just isn't on their radar.'

'No, I get that. But artists are not suddenly going to start charging ten or twenty pounds for something that took them weeks or months to do.'

'And I wouldn't expect them to, but there has to be some middle ground. We have to encourage more people to come and buy or the place will close.'

He frowned. 'Is that what Audrey said?'

'I have six months to somehow turn this place around or she will sell it. There's been hotel developers sniffing around for years so I presume she'd sell to one of those and wash her hands of it.'

'I wish she'd told me. I have a bit of money squirrelled away, I could have helped her out if I'd known she was in trouble.'

Audrey knew about his finances, why hadn't she told him? Although Audrey was one of the few people in his life who didn't see him as a free meal ticket.

'I don't think throwing money at it is the answer. It's not going to help long term,' Flick said. 'We have to find a way to make the studios self-sufficient or we'll be back here again in a few months once the money runs out.'

'No, you're probably right.'

'I need to have a meeting with everyone tomorrow, see if we can come up with a plan together.'

Luke shook his head. 'I'm not sure how that will be received. Many of the artists are stuck in their ways.'

'Then you'll have to help me persuade them that change is the only answer, or they lose this place for good.'

He nodded. 'I'll help.'

He had to do something to save this place before he left, for his mum and for the legacy left behind by Flick's grandad. But maybe he could help Flick realise her dreams too.

CHAPTER THREE

Flick woke up the next day and pulled back the curtains. She propped herself up against the headboard and looked out over the spectacular view. It was so much more beautiful in the daylight, the summer sunshine making everything sparkle. The sea was a stunning turquoise green today. The houses of all different colours were snuggled up together on the opposite hillside overlooking the little harbour. Lovegrove Bay had always been one of her favourite places. She wanted to walk around the pretty village, try one of the unique flavours of ice cream from the little shop on the corner of Main Street, eat fish and chips on the steps of the harbour, maybe even have a paddle on Blossom Beach.

But there was work to be done. She wanted to have a good look at each of the artists' shops, see how their space was laid out. Maybe presentation was the key or at least part of it.

Six months didn't feel like a very long time to turn around the shops' successes.

She thought about her conversation with Luke last night. She felt so frustrated that her nan hadn't told the artists what the lie of the land was. They had no idea why she was here, or the state of the studio's finances or that the whole place might be closed and bulldozed to the ground in a few months. At least if her nan had had that discussion with them they might have been more open to her coming in and changing everything. Audrey hated confrontation or breaking bad news. She was the classic ostrich, burying her head in the sand and hoping anything bad would go away. So now it was down to Flick. Her nan hadn't made it easy for her.

She bit her lip as she thought more about the conversation on the roof terrace. She couldn't help but smile when she remembered Luke doing the flying scene from *Titanic* with her. He was unashamedly silly and she loved that. She thought back to her previous boyfriends and whether any of them would have done something silly like that with her and the answer was definitely not.

She wanted someone she could have fun with. She knew life wasn't always sunshine and roses. There was a lot more to a relationship than having someone who made you laugh. A good relationship was being there for each other throughout the highs and lows but the lows were a little bit easier to deal with if you had someone you could be silly with. Luke made her laugh and she really liked that. It was just a shame he was leaving in a few weeks.

There had even been a moment when she'd turned around from *flying* over the sea when she'd thought he might kiss her. She'd seen his eyes cast down to her lips and she thought he was going to but then he stepped back and she decided she'd probably imagined it. He didn't know her, why would he kiss her? What would she have done if he had kissed her? She'd been flying so high that he'd joined in with her silliness she would have probably kissed him back. But god that would have made things awkward when they had to work together and live together. They were probably better off as friends, especially as he was leaving, so why did she feel a little bit disappointed about that?

She went out into the communal living area but there was no sign of Luke. His bedroom door was open and he wasn't in there. The bathroom door was closed, however, and she certainly didn't want a repeat of yesterday and to walk in on him naked again. She hoped he would have the good sense to lock the bathroom door.

She walked up to it and knocked. There was no answer. She called out to him but again there was no answer. But that didn't help her feel any more confident about opening the door, knowing that he liked to listen to music on his headphones.

She clamped one hand over her eyes and opened the door. There was still no sound from the other side.

So she moved forward and waved her arm around to

make sure the space was empty and there was still no noise or any evidence that someone was there.

'What are you doing?' came Luke's voice from behind her.

She whirled round with her hand still over her eyes and felt her other hand smash into his stomach.

'Ooof.'

'Sorry.'

She risked a peep through her fingers to see him doubled over, but at least he was fully clothed this time.

'I'm so sorry, I was just checking to see if anyone was in the bathroom. I didn't want to see you naked again.'

He straightened, rubbing his stomach gingerly. He wasn't wearing his glasses today, she wondered if he wore contact lenses or maybe they were just reading glasses. She tried to decide whether he was sexier with or without them and decided they both had their merits.

'It's OK.' His voice was strained. 'I just got back from a run and when I came in I saw you flapping your arms around in here, I thought it was some kind of weird dance. I'm also very glad I wasn't naked and on the receiving end of your flailing arms. I might have lost the ability to have children for good. But, just so you know, there is a lock on the bathroom door which I always use so with any luck you won't be seeing me naked ever again. Well unless…' he trailed off.

'Unless?'

'Well unless we're both naked,' he blushed furiously.

'Why would we both be naked?'

'Just forget I said anything. There won't be any more nakedness. Ever.'

She smirked as she realised what he'd been trying not to say. Enjoying his embarrassment, she decided to push it. 'You mean, mutually agreed nakedness.'

'I was just trying to cover all eventualities, but obviously *that* isn't going to happen. And I don't want it to. *That* isn't even on the table. I don't mean that we'd be doing it on the table. Or anywhere. Or at all. Ever. Jesus, I don't want to have sex with you. I have no idea why I said that about us both being naked. Can we just store that in the "never happened" box along with you walking in on me naked and me examining my penis in the mirror? Christ, why am I bringing that up again?'

Flick stared at him and burst out laughing. 'Oh, I'm going to like being friends with you. Completely platonic, non-naked friends who definitely won't be having sex ever.'

He flushed again and rolled his eyes. 'You can see why I'm single.'

'You're fine, don't worry about it. I'm going to have a shower, I will be locking the door so there won't be any more accidental nakedness and then you can help me face the troops.'

'Well, I have to have a shower too. Alone and behind locked doors. But then I'll be ready to help you.'

She smiled and closed the door, shaking her head. There was something so damned likeable about Luke Donnelly.

Flick made her way downstairs and started walking round the different rooms before the artists arrived. It had been a while since she'd been here but not a lot had changed. Same layout, same decor, even the threadbare carpet and rugs in the halls were the same. But now she was trying to look at it all through the eyes of potential customers.

The house had a kind of open-plan feel in that none of the individual shops or artists' rooms had doors, windows or walls to separate them from the rest of the house. There were just rooms, open spaces or tucked-away nooks where the artists had taken up residence.

In one room, there were beautifully embroidered quilts of various sizes and colours. The work was exquisite, not just the sewing and quilting, but the beautifully embroidered flowers, birds and animals too. But apart from two or three hanging on the walls, they weren't displayed nicely at all. There was a pile of them on the table and another pile on the floor. One work-in-progress was laid out on a large desk.

There were prices on the two quilts on the wall but none on any of the others. Flick knew how some people hated asking how much something was and would rather walk out than bother someone for a price. Although the old adage of 'If you have to ask you probably can't afford it' was probably true judging by the prices of the two on the walls. She had no doubt that the quilts on the wall had taken many days or even weeks to finish and that they were almost certainly worth the exorbitant price tag, but who could afford to buy something like that? Judging by the huge piles of quilts stacked up around the room, Ethel, the quilting artist, hadn't sold one for a very long time. There had to be some middle ground here. Flick didn't want to undersell what her work was worth but she somehow had to appeal to the average person. Ethel was clearly good at embroidery as well as quilting, perhaps she could make some very small, embroidered items to sell alongside the quilts like cushion covers or brooches.

Flick wandered down the hall to what was Aidan, the potter's, room. There were no plates, bowls or cups in here though. The room was filled with beautiful clay sculptures of various sizes, none of which had been made in moulds, all one-off, unique creations, although there were a lot of dragons. In fact probably seventy-five percent of the stock, if not more, were dragons which would have been perfect if a customer loved dragons, but there wasn't a lot of choice for those non-dragon-loving customers. She looked at the price tag of one of the medium-sized dragons and winced. She really was going to struggle to get the artists on side with offering cheaper products.

The next room was filled with gorgeous mosaics. Boats, sunsets, animals, famous landmarks all depicted with beautiful jewel-coloured bits of tile or glass. The room sparkled and gleamed as the mosaics caught the sunshine streaming through the windows. Every mosaic was displayed beautifully in here too, the perfect place to catch the sun. They were all priced clearly as well, Katherine had done a superb job with her presentation, but again a quick look at the prices showed the average person wouldn't be able to buy them, no matter how well the store was presented.

Flick moved to the next room which was where Rose did her paintings. It was clear she had an exceptional talent, especially for different landscapes. They were beautifully detailed, capturing the colours of nature so perfectly some of them could easily be mistaken for photos. There were a few paintings of dogs too. But the cheapest painting she could find was over eight hundred pounds, while the others were well into the thousands.

She wandered back out into the hall. Apart from Luke's studio space at the front of the house there were no other shops and there was still so much space that could be filled with other artists, two areas on this floor and a whole floor above them that was empty. Maybe more artists selling different and unusual wares would attract more people to the studios. She also wondered if reopening the café would be a viable option. Her nan had told her she could do whatever she wanted in the six months, but opening a café and then leaving again once her nan came home might be an unwelcome burden for her nan. Though if she could get someone to run that side of things then maybe her nan wouldn't see it as a burden at all, especially if it was doing well.

Flick walked down the hall to Luke's studio to find he was already there tweaking a life-size wooden carving of a great stag. The detail was incredible, the fine lines of fur, the velvet of the antlers, even the eyes looked real and alert.

'This is beautiful.'

He looked up and smiled. 'Thank you.'

'You have a wonderful talent.'

'It's something I love doing, I get lost in this for hours.'

'I totally get that. Do you always work here?'

'Pretty much. Sometimes I work outside in the summer or if the weather's nice, especially if I'm using a chainsaw or any other machinery.'

'I'd imagine people would get a big kick out of seeing you use a chainsaw to carve your sculptures. That's an attraction right there. The women especially would love it: rugged man using a chainsaw to carve wood, that's got sex appeal written all over it.'

Luke burst out laughing. 'I've never heard anyone say that about me before. I suppose you'd want me to be topless, wear a tight pair of jeans?'

'What can I say, sex sells.'

Luke laughed and shook his head. 'Apart from the very obvious health and safety problems with using a chainsaw while topless, well, I'm not sure if you noticed my body when you saw me naked, but there's a definite lack of a six-pack to impress the women.'

'You have a nice body, you might not have a six-pack but you have nice muscles.'

'I'm not sure *nice* is the compliment you want it to be.'

'Sometimes a man doesn't have to be some Greek

Adonis to be sexy or attractive, you could be doing something sexy like cuddling a baby or a puppy or carving some wood with a chainsaw.'

'So the only way *I* could be sexy is by cuddling a puppy with one hand and chainsaw carving with the other.'

'I didn't mean that… I'm making it worse, aren't I?'

'A little bit.'

'You have very attractive qualities.'

'Qualities?'

'You have nothing to be shy about, that's all I'm saying.' There was an awkward silence between them. 'I don't mean… that.' She gestured to his crotch.

'So I should be shy about my… tackle?' Luke asked, a smile twitching on his lips.

'Can we stop talking about your… manhood? I'd really prefer not to remember it.'

'Why was it offensive? Hideous? Malformed?'

Flick laughed. 'Will you stop?'

Luke held his hands up to show he was stopping.

This man made her smile so damn much. 'You know, funny men are very attractive too.'

His eyebrows shot up at that. 'I don't think that's true.'

'Oh it is. We like to laugh.'

'So while we're making love, you'd like me to crack a few jokes?'

She stared at him her eyes wide.

He cleared his throat. 'Hypothetically.'

'Umm, I don't think laughing during sex is necessarily a bad thing as long as we're laughing with each other not at each other.'

Luke weighed it up. 'I'll give you that.'

'But being around someone who makes you smile or laugh can only be a good thing. Last night, when you stood on the rooftop and pretended to fly with me, that made me laugh so much.'

'You found that attractive?'

'Honestly, yes. I couldn't stop thinking about it last night and this morning.'

He stared at her and she looked at the stag for want of something to do, her cheeks flushing.

'Anyway, can we get back on topic?' she said. 'Do you get many people coming up here to watch you work, you or the other artists?'

'Not really, the odd tourist in the summer, the odd rambler caught in the rain.'

'So we're not even getting people through the doors to look at your goods.'

'*My* goods?' Luke teased.

'Stop,' Flick laughed.

'No, footfall is very low.'

She sighed and looked around his studio. 'You haven't got a lot of stock here.'

'Most of my work is commission based. I do a few medium-sized table-top sculptures that I sell on Etsy or my website when time allows. My website has pictures of all my past sculptures so people can see my work there and see if I'm suitable for any commissions they might have in mind.'

'But if the odd tourist or rambler comes in here and there are no sculptures for them to look at, they can't buy anything or see your work.'

'That's true. I guess I could print out some pictures and put them in a folder for people to look at. But I am leaving in a few weeks.'

She decided to bypass that; he couldn't just do nothing for the next four weeks. 'It would be better if you actually had stock on the shelves for people to pick up and touch.'

'I'm not sure I have time to create surplus stock.'

'It wouldn't be surplus if people were buying it.'

'No one comes up here to buy anything. If they do, they soon find out it's too expensive.'

'But if you were to do smaller sculptures, say the size of a large mug or pint glass, sell them for twenty or thirty pounds, you would get more sales.'

'This level of detail on a pint-sized sculpture would still take several days and would be worth more than twenty pounds.'

'You could *not* do this level of detail on the smaller sculptures.'

'You mean, make them substandard?'

Flick sighed. She could understand his reasoning but if she couldn't get the artists to try and help themselves then nothing would change. And Luke's reaction to her suggestion was a good indication of how the other artists would react when she called a meeting later this morning. She wasn't looking forward to it.

Luke was just finishing shaping one of the stag's antlers, his mind filled with Flick. If she was going to ask the artists to produce smaller, substandard pieces of work, they were going to slaughter her. He was pretty annoyed by it himself, except he knew it was coming from a good place, a need to save the studios. If no one was selling anything they had to change.

He sighed. To be honest, she was just too damned likeable for him to be angry at her. And it wasn't just that she had no idea who he was, there was just something about her that he felt drawn to. She was sunshine after months of rain. He wanted to wrap himself up in her warmth, bask in it, and he hadn't felt like that for a long time. He loved how she made him smile so much. She was right when she'd said the night before that they shared a connection. It was something that was rare and didn't come along very often.

And it couldn't have come at a more inconvenient time – he was leaving in a few weeks. He couldn't exactly change his plans, he'd bought a house, he'd paid the builders to start work on it the day after he'd got the keys. He was excited about this new start. These feelings were just a blip. The whole move had been incredibly stressful with one problem after another to solve. It felt like, if there was such a thing as fate, it was conspiring against him getting his dream home in Scotland. But now he had exchanged contracts, it finally felt like it was within his reach. This was just another small problem to get past. So he would be professional, friendly and he'd do everything he could to help Flick save the studios and realise her dreams and then he could leave without looking back. He ignored the voice in his head that said that was going to be harder than he thought.

Just then the front door opened and his friend Quinn walked in. He was sweaty and had clearly been for a run over the hills. Luke moved over to the sink and poured him a glass of water, then walked back to his friend and handed it to him.

'Cheers mate,' Quinn said, taking a long drink. Luke had known Quinn for a few years now. They'd both started off working at the craft market on the village green selling their wares. Quinn was a metal worker and made sculptures or more recently monsters from household items like cutlery or tools. They were cute and people loved them. Their tables always seemed to be next to each other in the market and they just hit it off. Quinn was laid-back and made Luke laugh. They'd go for a pint once or twice a month and put the world to rights.

Quinn handed the empty glass back. 'Is it me or is that wonky tree out there looking a bit more wonky than normal?'

'I thought that the other day too. I'll have to get someone up here to have a look at those straps and chains that hold it up. Maybe it might need a bit more reinforcing.'

'It looks like one strong gust of wind and the whole

thing would go. Oh, did Audrey's granddaughter get here OK?' Quinn asked.

'Yes,' Luke said and was surprised by how exasperated he sounded in just that one word.

'Oh-oh, that doesn't sound good. Is she a pain in the arse?'

'No, Flick is lovely.' He rolled his eyes because now he sounded wistful.

'Oh.' Quinn was clearly confused. Luke didn't blame him. But then the penny dropped. 'Ohhhh. You like her.'

'No, that's not it. She's nice, that's all.'

He cursed himself that he was now using the word *nice* after telling Flick that it wasn't really a compliment. And she was so much more than that. *Nice* was doing her a disservice.

'So you're wondering how to navigate this because you're leaving?' Quinn asked.

'There's no navigation. I'm leaving in a few weeks, I don't need any complications and I certainly don't want to hurt her. We're friends, that's it.'

'But she's got under your skin.'

'No, not at all.' He sighed because there was no point in lying. 'Yes, she has.'

'Ha, I knew it.'

Just then Flick walked past, stopping when she saw Quinn and coming into the studio.

'Hello, are you interested in a piece of woodwork?' Flick asked, a smile lighting up her face, clearly delighted to have a customer.

'Umm... yes,' Quinn said, giving Luke a panicked look.

'Well, while we don't have a lot of stock here today for you to look at, we do have lots of photos on Luke's website.' She pulled her phone from her pocket and she must have already been looking him up as she found his website very quickly. She started showing Quinn some photos of Luke's work. 'You can see the workmanship is exquisite, the level of detail is beautiful. You can see his experience is not just with animals but with people too so, whatever it is you want, Luke will be able to capture it exactly as you imagine it, only better.'

'Yes, these are very good,' Quinn said, still passing Luke looks of alarm.

Luke sighed. 'Flick, Quinn is my friend, he's not here to buy my art.'

'You aren't?' she frowned. 'Then why did you say you were?'

'Sorry,' Quinn grinned. 'I wasn't sure if Luke would get into trouble from the new boss for chatting not working.'

Flick laughed. 'Have you made me out to be some kind of dragon lady already?'

'No, he said you were very nice,' Quinn said.

'Nice,' she said, pretending to be outraged and for good reason after Luke had complained about her use of that word earlier.

He cleared his throat. 'You have... qualities.'

She laughed loudly. 'Right, I'm going. Quinn, nice to meet you. Luke, get back to work.'

He smiled as he watched her go and he was still stupidly smiling long after he heard her footsteps disappear.

'She's lovely,' Quinn said.

'Yeah she is.'

'Oh dear god, you have it bad. You want my advice?'

'Not really.'

'Live for now, my friend, live life with no regrets. Worry about the future when it gets here.'

'Are you saying I should just sleep with her and then leave? Casual sex really isn't my thing.'

Even if that was on offer, which he highly doubted.

'There was nothing casual about the way you two were looking at each other. And I'm not saying you should do that. I'm saying enjoy the next few weeks and find out if you have anything worth fighting for. It could be over very quickly once you sleep together.'

'Oh, thanks very much.'

'I didn't mean that. I just meant sometimes there is a spark and it's just sexual, it goes out once you've done the deed. Like eating a really nice slice of chocolate cake – sometimes, no matter how nice it is, you couldn't possibly eat another slice.'

'And what happens if that spark ignites a fire that never goes out?'

'Well that definitely sounds like something you would fight for.'

'That's what I'm worried about.'

Quinn stared at him in disbelief. 'Are you seriously telling me you don't want to get involved with this woman in case she turns out to be the love of your life and that would be too inconvenient?'

'No, of course not.'

But if Luke was being completely honest with himself, he wasn't avoiding starting anything with Flick because he thought it would end in marriage and babies and a happy ever after. It was because he knew he could fall in love with her very easily and that would only lead to him getting hurt when she inevitably didn't feel the same way.

Quinn wasn't to be deterred. 'Let me tell you, real love only comes around once in your life, if you're lucky. If you have the slightest inkling that this could be that for you, then grab hold of it with both hands. And if it isn't, well at least you'll have fun finding out.'

Quinn made it sound so simple but it wasn't. Even if Luke wanted to pursue something with Flick, it was highly unlikely she'd want to take that step with him.

CHAPTER FOUR

Flick waited nervously in the old café for the artists to arrive for their meeting. She'd been round to them all and introduced herself and told them there would be a meeting today. Some of them had looked at her warily as if she was going to come in and change everything about their happy little status quo. She was dreading telling them that that was exactly what she was here to do.

She had bought some nice biscuits and cakes from a little bakery in the town and hoped that would go some way to placate them. One by one they filtered in, eyeing her and the cakes suspiciously. Flick thought that her nan had probably never called a meeting before. She definitely hadn't told Luke about the financial problems Waterfall House was facing, even though she lived with him, so it was very unlikely the other artists knew either.

She glanced around at their faces. Her nan had told

her they wouldn't like change and she could see they already had their defences up. Luke gave her an encouraging smile which made her feel fractionally better.

'Thank you all for coming,' Flick said.

'Not sure we had much choice,' Aidan muttered.

'Shut up, this is important,' Luke said.

Everyone looked at Luke in surprise. Clearly they weren't used to him speaking up but Flick was grateful for it. Although she was capable of defending herself, she decided to ignore it and press on, not wanting to antagonise anyone just yet.

'I'm not sure how much my nan has told you but Waterfall House is in trouble. The way I understand it is that none of you pay any rent here but you have an arrangement where you pay twenty-five percent of any sale to my nan. But there aren't any sales, not one single sale since Christmas, for anyone, and last year wasn't much better. So no money is coming in and, while the mortgage on this place was paid off many years ago, there are still bills and overheads. Some of you may know that she sold her house in the town a few years ago and moved in here and has been using the money to pay the bills for this place ever since. That money has now run out and, in true Audrey style, she's been burying her head in the sand and hoping something miraculous would happen. She's now run away to Australia for six months and left me to deal with it.'

Flick knew that sounded harsh but this was her nan all over. She loved her nan but Audrey was a dreamer not a doer.

'We've now reached a turning point. We have six months to turn this place around or my nan will sell it.'

There was a gasp from Rose. 'Waterfall House has always been here.'

'I know but it's not making any money. The café isn't in use so we're not getting any money from that and there's only five artists here when there used to be so many more. By the sounds of it, my nan has given up on the place. She said a developer has been after her for years to turn this place into a hotel and my nan has reached the point where she's willing to let him if we can't do something to save it.'

'Can't you do something?' Katherine said to Luke, which Flick thought was odd.

'As Flick said last night when I offered to help, throwing money at it isn't the answer, we need to think about a long-term solution here. We need to be the ones to change.'

'What do you have in mind?' Ethel said, folding her arms across her chest as if she would say no to anything that was proposed.

'Firstly, I want to say that your work is stunning,' Flick said. 'All of you. I had a good look around your shops this morning before you arrived and the quality of the work is exceptional. That is not the reason for our lack of sales but some of your rooms or shops could be presented better. For some of you your area is just a workspace, not a space for showcasing your wonderful art. I'd like you all to look at Katherine's studio and see how her space is laid out. Every mosaic is displayed beautifully with clear prices on all of them, they aren't stacked up in piles with no prices. Some of you don't have any stock at all. You need to think about what your space looks like to potential customers and whether it appeals to them.'

'I suppose we can do that,' Rose said.

'Some of you need to diversify. Aidan, your sculptures are stunning but most of them are dragons.'

'I like dragons,' Aidan said, grumpily.

'And that's great for fellow dragon lovers, but some people might prefer to see a dolphin, a deer, a puppy or an eagle. Could we try doing some other animals, alongside the dragons of course?'

'I'll think about it.'

Flick ploughed on. 'Rose, your landscapes are lovely but maybe you could also paint some animals, portraits of celebrities, pets, flowers just to try to appeal to a wider audience.'

'I suppose.'

'Footfall, or rather the lack of it, is one of our biggest problems. We need to give people a reason to come up here. To that end I want to reopen the café. Well, not me personally, I don't know the first thing about serving food, but I'll find someone to run it. If people are up here for a coffee they might be inclined to wander round your studios. We could even offer a voucher, say five percent off to spend on your art for every time they spend twenty pounds or more in the café.'

'I'm not sure I want my work discounted,' Katharine said. 'It devalues it.'

'It's only five percent,' Luke said.

'For every customer who spends twenty pounds. That's a lot of customers.'

'It's also a lot more customers than you're getting right now,' Luke said.

Katherine pulled a face and muttered something under her breath.

'I'd like to give them other reasons to come up here,' Flick went on. 'The fact that you create your masterpieces here and that this is a working studio is one of its attributes. I'd like a day a week where you'd be demonstrating your work and we'll advertise it to try to encourage people to come up here. That could be every Saturday for example and it would be a demonstration day for everyone, or we could have a quilt demonstration day on the Monday, wood carving demonstration on the Tuesday for example. People can ask questions and talk to you about your process. How would you feel about that?'

'Do you want us all to be topless?' Luke teased.

'I beg your pardon,' Ethel said.

'It was a joke, Ethel, just a joke about something me and Flick were talking about earlier. No one will be topless.'

'I should think not. No one has seen these breasts for forty years since my husband passed. I'm not going to whip them out just to sell a few quilts.'

'No one is asking you to do that,' Flick said, passing Luke a glare.

'I think it's a great idea,' Luke said, quickly. 'People

55

love that kind of thing, watching someone work, and it really gives them an appreciation of how much work goes into one of our pieces. And it's only one day a week, what harm can it do?'

'I don't work well with people staring at me,' Rose said.

'I'm not really a people person,' Aidan said.

'You kind of have to be if you want to sell your work. Or at least pretend to be,' Flick said.

None of them looked particularly happy about this. Flick wondered if this was part of the reason for the lack of footfall: grumpy faces and bad attitudes.

'We need more artists too. If you know anyone who offers something different to what is already here, then please ask them to contact me and we can discuss getting them a space,' Flick said.

She looked around at them. None of her suggestions was being met with joy right now, so she was dreading saying what she knew she had to say next.

'I also think we need to offer something that the average person can afford to buy. Most people do not have enough money to spend three thousand pounds on a painting.'

'I'm not lowering my prices,' Rose said.

'Me neither,' Katherine said and Aidan shook his head vehemently.

'I'm not expecting you to. As I said, all of your work is exquisite and I'm sure more than deserving of the price tag. But Rose, for example, you could offer prints of your work for a fraction of the price. You could even look into getting some of your paintings printed on mugs, bags, t-shirts, mouse mats, the options are endless. That doesn't compromise your work but it makes it more accessible for the average person. Katherine, you could do smaller mosaics, coasters for example, pots, tree decorations. Aidan, you could do mugs, plates and bowls for example, or very small versions of your brilliant sculptures. Luke, you could do the same. Ethel, your embroidery is beautiful, you could offer some personalised embroidery like an initial or a name, you could embroider pictures of animals. I can advertise our working studios, do Facebook or Instagram ads, put notices up on local online forums. But there's no point encouraging people to come up here if they can't afford anything.'

'You want us to produce tat for the tourists?' Ethel said, distastefully.

'I want you to get some sales, because surely twenty-five pounds is better than nothing?'

'It will still take a lot of our time to make things like this, even on a smaller scale,' Aidan said. 'My time and skill are worth more than twenty-five pounds.'

Rose nodded. 'Even the smallest canvas, say four by five inches, would easily be fifty pounds to reflect my level of skill and experience.'

'Maybe you could not put so much time and effort into the smaller pieces,' Flick tried.

The looks around the room were scandalised.

'Look, we have to do something,' Luke said. 'Audrey has basically been funding this place, single-handedly for years, with little to nothing from us. She sold her house in the town to continue paying for it. And we all know why. This was her husband's dream. A place to help people with brain injuries with art and somewhere for artists to work and create their art. It's time we gave something back. And let's face it, if this place closes, you're never going to find another studio space that doesn't charge anything for rent or other bills. Clearly none of us *need* the money or we would have realised we had to change our way of working years ago. So we have to make a choice, pack up and find studio space somewhere else if your integrity means so much to you, or come up with some kind of compromise. Flick has come up with some great suggestions to sell cheaper pieces and I really think you need to consider them. It doesn't mean you have to stop doing the bigger stuff that you all love doing, but you need to come up with something that brings some money in too.'

They all grumbled and muttered between them. Flick really hoped none of them would take Luke's first option and pack up and leave. A working studio with no artists would be even harder to save. But then again, with such favourable conditions, she could probably persuade other artists to come in their place. Maybe that was what this place needed, some fresh blood. And if the conditions were clear from the start, that the artists had to produce cheaper alternatives alongside the more expensive stuff, then at least everyone would know where they stood and what was expected.

She took a deep breath because kicking out the resident artists was probably not part of her nan's plan for change but she had to do something to show them she was serious. 'I totally understand your reluctance to produce pieces of art that are less than your normal high quality and if you feel you need to leave rather than lower yourself to that, then we'll be sorry to see you go,' Flick said, feeling herself visibly shake at the prospect of kicking people out. But Luke was right, something had to change.

'So it's your way or the highway?' Aidan asked.

Her mouth was dry as she nodded. She hated confrontation. 'I'll come and see you all tomorrow just before closing and you can tell me what you've decided to do.'

Muttering angrily between themselves, everyone but Luke left.

She let out a heavy sigh. 'I really know how to make friends, don't I?'

'We don't need a friend right now. Audrey has played that role very well over the last few years and to what end? What we need now is a boss, someone who is going to take charge of this place and drag it, kicking and screaming, into something profitable.'

Flick nodded, knowing he was right but not feeling any better about it.

'Come on,' Luke said. 'I'll treat you to lunch, I know just the place.'

∽

If Flick had been hoping for a nice restaurant or even a friendly local café she would have been disappointed. As it was her head was swirling with everything that had just happened in the meeting. She kept thinking about what she could have said differently and what else she could do to save the house so she had no hopes or expectations at all for lunch. She wasn't even sure she could eat, her stomach was churning so much. But when Luke walked up to a little yellow food truck, similar in size to an ice cream van, and ordered a burger and fries, she was a little bit surprised.

'What would you like?' Luke asked, fishing out his wallet.

She looked up at the menu for a moment before she shook her head, not really seeing the words. 'I'll have the same.'

'It'll be a few minutes. Why not grab a seat and I'll bring it over to you when it's ready,' said a young, redheaded woman.

Luke nodded. 'Thanks Polly.'

He gestured to a nearby picnic bench and they sat down opposite each other.

'How are you doing?' Luke asked.

'It's definitely a tough crowd.'

'They've been stuck in their ways for years with no one telling them they have to do anything different.'

'I think fresh blood could be the answer. People who are young and enthusiastic.'

'I don't know. Artists are a proud bunch, no matter how young they are, and many of them feel like their skills are above the kind of things you're asking them to do.'

She sighed. 'I think getting visitors up there is going to be half the battle. If they can see I'm doing that then maybe they'll be a bit more open to doing their part. I'd love to reopen the café if I could find someone to run it, it would bring a daily stream of visitors to the studios. But while we were in there for our meeting this morning, I felt like it needed some TLC. Not just cleaning, but some new countertops, maybe some new tables and chairs, a paint job. Some of the studios need a bit of love too, or at least some more shelves or tables to display their work on. Ethel's quilts are in a big pile on the floor.' She chewed her lip. 'Maybe we can hold a painting party, invite people up here to help with the painting in return for free pizza.' She sighed, she didn't think many people would give up their time just for some pizza.

'There is a small kitty of money,' Luke said. 'If there is some decorating or any repairs that need doing, especially with your plans to reopen the café, there is a bit of money to do any renovations with.'

'Oh my nan never mentioned that. I got the impression she didn't have any money at all.'

'It's just for any improvements or repairs. So let me know what you need and I'll get it for you or arrange it. I know a lot of local tradespeople so I can get jobs done quite quickly.'

Flick felt herself brighten at the prospect of smartening up the place. 'I'll make a list today.'

She looked around. They were on the far side of the village green, which was surrounded by brightly coloured shops and houses. She was surprised to see pirate flags flying from every tree, lamppost and shop window. There were skeletons in cages, parrots perched on top of lamp posts, and cannons dotted around the green that certainly hadn't been there when she used to come here as a child.

'What's with all the pirate stuff?'

'Oh, we have our annual pirate festival on Saturday, everyone dresses up, there's skirmishes on the boats, cannons being fired and lots of bands singing sea shanties. It's a lot of fun. Well, for half the town. The other half all roll their eyes and laugh at grown adults dressing up.'

'Which half are you?'

He closed one eye and hooked a finger. 'Arrr,' he growled.

She laughed.

Polly came over then with two trays laden with burgers and fries. They both thanked her and she went back to the van.

Flick tucked into her burger. 'Oh my god, this is amazing.'

Luke grinned. 'I know, Bumblebees does the best burgers in Lovegrove Bay.'

Flick popped a chip in her mouth. 'These are great too, crispy, fluffy and perfectly seasoned.'

'I think she uses paprika.'

'They're delicious.'

'Polly is a culinary queen. She does the best bacon or sausage sandwiches in the mornings for breakfast, and burgers, baked potatoes and other sandwiches for lunch. A lot of people just come here for the fries. She does great hot chocolates too, with lots of different flavours. Coffees and teas too of course.'

'Do you think she wants a job running a café?' Flick joked.

Luke paused with a chip halfway to his mouth. 'Why don't you ask her? Her Bumblebee van is a bit limited in terms of size and its cooking capabilities but it's flexible, she can take it wherever she wants and Waterfall House is a little bit out of the way so not as much footfall as she gets down here. But we used to get loads of visitors up there when the café *was* open so maybe being out the way won't matter with the right person running the place.'

Flick swallowed her mouthful of burger as she stared at him. She wasn't sure whether Polly would go for it, but there was only one way to find out. As Polly was clearing away the rubbish from the next table, Flick waved her over.

'Is everything OK with the food?' Polly asked, as she walked closer.

'Everything is great. Better than great actually. We were wondering if you wanted a job?'

Polly looked at her in surprise. 'A catering job?'

'I'm from Waterfall House, up on Waterfall Hill.'

'The House with the Wonky Tree? Yes, I know it.'

'I'm Audrey's granddaughter and I'm taking over the

management of the place. We want to reopen the café and we'd like you to run it.'

Polly blinked in surprise.

'It'd be totally yours to do with what you want. But really we'd like the same kind of thing you're doing here, bacon and sausage sandwiches for breakfast, burgers, chips, baked potatoes and sandwiches for lunch, maybe some cakes. Though if you wanted to do something more elaborate that would be fine too.'

'What are your terms? Am I renting the place off you or are you employing me and paying me a wage?'

Flick cursed that she hadn't really thought this through. She certainly didn't have any money to employ her and she didn't want to have to think about sorting out national insurance or anything else as an employer.

'The place would be yours, just like the van,' Luke said, looking at Flick to see if she agreed.

Flick nodded.

'I lease the van.'

'Well, there would be no rent or overheads to pay at the café,' Luke went on. 'All income would be yours for the first two months which will give you enough time to establish yourself and get it up and running. After that, you'd pay us twenty-five percent just like the artists do when they sell one of their pieces.'

Polly stared at them, considering their offer, then she looked at the van fondly, painted bright yellow with bees and flowers round the sides. 'I love my little bumblebee van.'

Flick's heart sank. Of course it wouldn't be that easy.

'But I've always dreamed of having my own café or restaurant one day – although I'm not sure if Waterfall House is the right place for me.'

'Maybe you could use the experience of running a bigger place, see what you would do if you had your own place one day,' Flick said. 'I have to be honest, reopening the café is our last-ditch attempt at saving the studios. If we can't make a profit for the studios in six months, the place will be sold,' she added. 'And I know that isn't a great incentive but at least if you gave us six months and you didn't like it, it's not a big commitment. You could even keep the van and just work in the café in the mornings and then come back down here in your van for the lunchtime rush, or work in the café three or four days a week and use the van on other days.'

'We'll pay for all your food and supplies for the first two months,' Luke added. 'After that it will have to come out of your income.'

Polly chewed her lip. 'I need to think about this.'

'I understand,' Luke said. 'But we do need someone to start as soon as possible. Why don't you come up to the café this afternoon, once you've finished here, and we can show you around and you can see if it's somewhere you'd like to work. Also if the café needs any utensils or... blenders or coffee machines or anything else you can think of, we can make a list of things we'll get, within reason, to make the place work for you. No pressure, or commitment, just come and have a look.'

She nodded. 'OK, but just a look. It's not a yes.'

'Of course,' Flick said, trying and failing not to get

her hopes up. 'We were going to give it a lick of paint too, so if there's a colour scheme that works for you, you could let us know about that as well.'

Polly smiled cautiously. 'I'll see you this afternoon.'

With that she returned to her van.

'What do you think, will she do it?' Flick asked as she returned her attention to her delicious burger.

'I don't know. I think she'd be perfect but it's a big change and not necessarily the best thing for her.'

Flick smiled. 'Did you bring me down here because you thought she would be a good fit?'

He grinned. 'Maybe. You said you wanted someone to run the café, Polly has the skills and the experience. I thought it would be good for the two of you to at least meet.'

'Crafty.'

'Practical. When we get back, I want you to look at the shop space next door to the café. I think you should open a gift shop. People love a gift shop. There are catalogues that you can order gifts like scarves, gloves, cuddly toys, calendars, diaries, bird feeders from, that sort of thing. You buy them at cost price and sell them with a mark-up. You can source local foods like honey, jam, pickles, cheeses and sell those too. If you don't feel comfortable enough to have your own studio space to sell your wish jars, you could sell them in the shop. But mostly you could sell craft supplies: paints, brushes, canvases, embroidery threads, wool, crochet and knitting needles, clay, maybe little kits to make mosaics or everything you need to start painting, or fused glass kits, just as you imagined.'

'But I don't know the first thing about running a business.'

'You don't need to. You source stuff, you sell it, that's it. If stuff sells well you buy more, if it doesn't you don't. If people ask if you sell something you haven't got, tell them you can order it in and we'll find it somewhere. If lots of people ask for something like chocolate or candles, order some in and see if they sell well too. But at least, in some small way, you'd be living out your dreams to sell craft supplies.'

'You make it sound so simple.'

'It doesn't have to be hard.'

Flick wanted to protest. She couldn't run a shop. Could she?

'There's enough money in the kitty to buy some stock to start you off.'

'There is?'

'Yes, we can stretch to that. What have you got to lose? In six months Waterfall House could be gone so you might as well give it a go.'

She bit her lip as she thought, unable to come up with any more reasons why she shouldn't.

'I'll have a look. It's not a yes.'

He grinned. 'I understand.'

CHAPTER FIVE

Flick walked back through the studio, looking at it through new eyes. Now she knew there was a bit of money to do the place up, she needed to see what they could do with it. She didn't know how much was in the kitty and she didn't want to go crazy with suggesting improvements everywhere so she was going to create two lists: Need and Want.

The carpet in the area between the studios needed to be replaced. It was so tatty and threadbare she could see the wooden floor underneath poking through. There was no chance of being able to appreciate the different colours or patterns either as the carpet was a dirty shade of brown. She added it to her Need list.

The lights along the halls were very dated. They did their job but it would be more atmospheric to have something a bit more cool or retro. Maybe some light fittings that looked like old brass gas lamps or those lights made from old taps, or maybe even just some fairy lights. She added lights to the Want list.

She hovered on the edge of the mosaic studio, watching Katherine creating a much smaller mosaic scene of hills, rivers and trees. Even at this size, Flick could see there was a lot of work involved as she measured and cut the glass to the right size and shape. But Katherine was fast too, clearly with her skills and experience she could produce something much faster than someone just starting out. And that skill and experience should be reflected in the price.

Flick glanced around the room. There wasn't much that was needed in here, as every bit of wall space was taken up with beautiful mosaics.

She moved on to the next studio where Ethel, Rose and Aidan were talking in hushed, angry whispers. As she approached, Rose spotted her and shushed them. They all fell quiet and stared at her with contempt.

Flick didn't linger, hurrying past and going upstairs to the café. If they decided to stay, she would ask them what they wanted to update their spaces then, but the café was probably the most important, at least for now.

It definitely needed a lick of paint, she would let Polly choose the colour if she decided she wanted to be a part of it. The wooden floor was OK, probably just needed a good clean. The countertops, however, were peeling plastic and definitely could do with a big overhaul. In fact the tables and chairs probably needed replacing too.

She saw the archway that led through to another studio space, probably the area Luke had planned for the gift shop. She wandered through and looked around. It was quite a large area with shelves already fitted into the walls. There was also a large octagonal area in one corner of the room which was in the turret part of the house and a curved staircase that led up to a mezzanine level. There was even a little arched alcove where she could display her wish jars. It had character and there was a small, hopeful, excited part of Flick that could see herself there, selling all her craft supplies and sourcing cool gifts to sell in the shop.

Could she really do it? What did she have to lose? As Luke said, the studios might be gone in six months. She could easily run the gift shop and do the marketing for the studios too. And having a gift shop and selling craft supplies might help the studios as well.

'What do you think?'

She turned round to see Luke watching her from the doorway.

'I'm going to do it,' Flick blurted out before she could change her mind.

A smile spread across his face. 'I think you'll be perfect at it. I'll get you the link to the website where you can buy the gifts and you can choose your stock. Is there anything you want doing in here?'

She looked around. 'I'm obviously going to need some more shelves and tables for the middle of the room and the mezzanine area upstairs but I don't think it needs any renovations. Maybe just some fairy lights round the roof beams and the mezzanine railings. I could put fairy lights on the shelves too.'

'I can sort that out no problem.'

'I think our biggest outlay will be the café. It needs a paint job, new counters, tables and chairs and whatever machines or equipment Polly will need to make it work. I had thought about new carpets in the halls between the studios, but there's wooden floor underneath. I think if we ripped up the carpet and just had the floor cleaned and polished, it would probably do the job. Then we can save the kitty money for the café and I guess the stock for the gift shop but I won't have a lot of stock to start with. I'll have to start small and build up from there.'

'You don't have to worry about not having enough in the kitty. There's probably more than you think and I can get things for the café pretty cheap, so please get what you want for the shop.'

Flick suddenly felt like a kid in a toy shop being told to buy whatever she wanted. She had so many ideas for the gift shop, all the different craft supplies and kits she could buy so people could have a go at making mosaics, or crochet or painting themselves. And she had lots of ideas for the kinds of gifts she wanted to sell too.

'You look excited?' Luke asked.

'Yeah, I am.'

'Good.'

She looked around the room, potential shining from every corner. She frowned as she glanced over at one corner of the room.

'You know, I used to play here as a child and I'm pretty sure this room had a secret room. Some kind of bookshelf that led to a little cupboard-type area.'

'Oh yeah, that's over here,' Luke said, leading the way to the corner she had looked at. 'It's not very big though, I'm not quite sure what the point of it was, unless it was purely put in to entertain small children with tales of secret passageways and smugglers and pirates hiding secret treasure.'

She smiled at the thought of Luke telling stories like that to small children.

'Luke!' a female voice called.

'Shit,' Luke muttered. 'Quick, in here.'

He grabbed her hand, flicked a little switch on the bookcase and as it swung open he bundled her inside, closing the bookcase behind them.

'What are you—' Flick started before Luke clamped a hand over her mouth. Her eyes widened in surprise.

The next moment she heard footsteps walk into the room. High-heeled footsteps by the sound of them as they strode across the wooden floor. 'Luke, are you in here?'

Flick looked up at Luke as he shook his head frantically, silently urging her to be quiet. She peered out through the tiny crack and could see a very pretty blonde woman walking round the room. Flick held her breath as the woman strode past the bookcase and started going upstairs to the mezzanine calling Luke's name again.

Luke released her mouth but put a finger over his

lips to tell her to keep quiet. They were standing very close. Luke was right, there was very little room in this little cubbyhole. In fact she could feel the warmth of his skin against hers, feel his breath on her face. She could see the tiny flecks of gold in his toffee-brown eyes and the dark stubble shading his chin. She was so acutely aware of his scent, which smelled like the tang of the sea on a summer's day, coupled with something sweet like apples. He smelled delicious. She really liked him. He was sweet, kind, funny, easy to talk to. She knew she could very easily fall for him. If only fate wasn't taking him away from her. She looked up at him and he was staring at her too. The world outside the cupboard seemed to fade away. Something sparked between them, a connection, a need, she wasn't sure what it was, but she felt sure he was going to kiss her and she was surprised by how much she wanted that.

She was vaguely aware of the woman coming back down the stairs and leaving the room but they were still staring at each other, his breath heavy, her heart racing. She felt him lean in towards her, or was she leaning in towards him? Either way their bodies were now touching.

Then he cleared his throat. 'I think she's gone, we can probably go back outside now.'

'Right, yes, of course.'

He swung the bookcase open and stepped out into the main room again. Flick brushed a hand through her hair, suddenly feeling awkward with him. Had she completely imagined the way he had been looking at her? She cast around the cubbyhole so she wouldn't have to look at him. 'You know, the secret room is much bigger than this.'

'What?'

'This little cubbyhole is just the entrance to it.' She felt around the back panel which was engraved with leaves. But she knew one of them was a button, she just couldn't remember which one it was. Finally she found it, pressed the leaf down like a little catch and the back panel swung open to reveal a small dusty room that still held the cushions she had laid on when she was a little child and was reading her favourite books. There was a small window that let in a shaft of sunlight and there was fairy lights wrapped around the shelves at the back, although currently unlit.

'Oh my god, how did I not know this was here?' Luke stepped into the room.

'It was well hidden.'

'Did your grandad make this for you?'

'I don't know, he just showed it to me one day when I came to stay. He said he'd found a secret room and you can imagine how excited I was about that. I never knew whether he'd found it like he said, or whether he built it for me. Knowing him, I wouldn't be surprised if he did build it. He had a lot of time for me, he was always playing with me or telling me one of his amazing stories.' She smiled sadly as she touched the fairy lights. 'It's been fifteen years since he died and I still miss him.'

'Sadly I never met Tom but I know he was a great man and his legacy of this place continues.'

'That's why I came down here to fight for it. This was his dream and maybe it was a silly dream, when a place like this has so many overheads, but I believe in it and I want to help it continue for many, many years to come.'

'I do too.'

She smiled at that and then turned to face him. 'So are you going to tell me why you threw me in a cupboard to hide from that woman?'

Luke let out a groan. 'Natalia. She wants to date me and won't take no for an answer. She comes up here all the time bringing cakes or asking me out or just blatantly sliding a condom into my hand and telling me she could show me a good time.'

Flick felt her eyebrows shoot up. 'That's bold.'

She couldn't help feeling a little bit impressed by that. Not the harassment, just the courage to go up to someone and do that. She couldn't even bring herself to kiss a man in a cupboard who was looking at her like he wanted to eat her in case she was rejected. And in this case, she had been right not to since he had awkwardly put an end to that little tête-à-tête and immediately distanced himself from her. But Natalia, with her swishing blonde hair, long legs and short skirt, had no such reservations. She was clearly used to getting any man she wanted and she'd set her sights on Luke which was an odd match.

Natalia looked the sort of woman who would want to be wined and dined in the most expensive and exclusive restaurants in the world. She'd be most at home in a top-of-the-range Porsche convertible with diamonds round her neck. Maybe Flick shouldn't judge a book by its cover but the woman had been carrying a Gucci handbag and was wearing the famous, red-soled shoes of Louboutin. A man like Luke couldn't fulfil those dreams for Natalia. He was wearing a t-shirt that had a hole in the shoulder, jeans that were probably ten years old or more and a tatty pair of trainers that probably didn't have any brand.

That wasn't to say he wasn't an attractive man – he was, with lovely warm eyes and a gorgeous smile. He had the kind of body that was perfect for a hug, solid, comforting. Nice strong arms too. He could take Flick out for fish and chips on the beach and she would be very happy with that. Except he'd backed away from that kiss so maybe she wasn't his type either.

'I don't mind bold, but she's not really interested in me, none of them are.'

'You have… multiple women chasing you and giving you condoms?'

'Not giving me condoms but yes I have a mini fan club,' Luke said, dryly. 'To be fair, the others just sidle up to me in the town if they see me, they don't make the effort that Natalia is putting in.'

'But if they're not interested in you, what are they interested in?'

'It doesn't matter. Shall we go to the café? I expect Polly will be there soon.'

She followed him out of the secret room, carefully shutting both doors behind her.

'Are you some kind of god of sex?' Flick asked. 'You can give women multiple orgasms simply by looking at them. You have a super-powered penis that sends all women into some kind of erotic frenzy. You've slept with one woman from the town who nearly died from multiple orgasms and now everyone wants a piece of you.'

Luke's cheeks flushed adorably. God, she really liked this man.

'That's it, isn't it?' Flick teased. 'You really are a god of sex?'

'I'm pretty sure all the women I've been with had a good time, I made sure of that, but I don't think anyone has ever called me a god of sex before. Just the regular, good kind of sex.'

She smirked at him downplaying his sexual capabilities. Any other man would have bragged about his sexual prowess. It was like Luke didn't know the rules of flirting. 'Surely this is your opportunity to say something like, *Baby I will rock your world*, not tell me your sex is the normal, regular kind.'

'Ah yes. Of course.' He cleared his throat. 'Yes, I'm a god of sex, that's why everyone wants to be with me. And if me and you ever get down to the, umm… rumpy-pumpy we'll be swinging from the chandeliers. How's that?'

Flick nodded, trying and failing to suppress her laughter.

'That was too much, wasn't it?' Luke said.

The laughter burst out into a snort. 'Rumpy-pumpy?'

'Well what am I supposed to call it?'

'Here, let me show you.' Flick pushed him up against the wall and ran a finger down the collar of his t-shirt touching the bare skin of his chest. 'When we make love for the first time, you'll be begging for mercy,' she said, softly.

He looked genuinely terrified.

'Was *that* too much?' Flick said, letting him go.

He cleared his throat. 'No… umm… a little.'

'It was better than offering to have rumpy-pumpy with someone,' Flick huffed.

'I'll give you that.'

There was the sound of someone clearing their throat, and they both looked up to see Polly watching them.

'Sorry, did I come at a bad time?'

'No, sorry we were just…' Flick trailed off. 'We were just messing around. This is not… We're not—'

'Thanks for coming,' Luke said, smoothly.

Since when was he the smooth one? Unless Polly was his type. Flick felt a stab of disappointment at that thought but quickly recovered herself. Having Polly here was for the greater good, even if that meant that Polly and Luke would be the ones swinging from the chandeliers.

'Let me show you around,' Flick said.

She moved into the café. 'Well this is the main area, seating for up to forty people. Behind the counter we have a… coffee machine.' Flick gestured to the great big monster of a machine. She had never worked in catering but even she could see this thing was old and dated. 'Umm, various cake cabinets.' Which definitely needed replacing. 'And through here is the kitchen and…' she trailed off when she saw the extent of the kitchen was a small seventies-style oven with built-in grill, a microwave and a toaster.

'Whatever you need to make this work, we can get,' Luke said, his eyes widening as he took in the lack of facilities for the first time. 'We can get everything cleaned or repainted. We had plans to replace the countertops and the tables and chairs but you tell us what you want and we'll get it sorted.'

To Flick's surprise, Polly didn't look disgusted or horrified. She looked excited. Flick smiled, recognising that look. It was the look she'd had a few minutes before when looking around the gift shop and seeing its potential, excited for what she could make it. And with Luke's offer of getting whatever Polly needed or wanted, Flick knew this was in the bag.

Polly rearranged her face into something more professional. 'This place needs a lot of work.'

'I know,' Luke said, sadly, clearly not realising that Polly had already decided she was going to do it. 'It's been closed for so long and the lack of facilities was a bone of contention for the last chef, which is why he left. But I figured you were used to working in much smaller conditions in your van with the bare minimum of facilities so if anyone was going to make this work, it was going to be you.'

Polly smiled at that.

'If I'm going to do this, I have a list of things I'd need,' she said, pulling out her tablet from her bag.

'Of course, whatever you need.'

Polly looked around and this time she wasn't able to hide her excitement.

Luke smiled. 'Is that a yes?'

Polly nodded, the smile growing on her own face. Luke let out a small sigh of relief.

'Let's get started then.' Luke gestured for her to go back out the kitchen and followed her to a table and chairs. They all sat down and Polly immediately pulled up a webpage showing various different kitchen appliances and utensils.

They started talking about what Polly wanted to do with the place, the colours, the tables, the layout of the counter and the kitchen, and Luke nodded and wrote everything down while Polly compiled a shopping list and then sent him a link to it. Flick watched the two of them chatting animatedly about Polly's plans and Polly getting more and more passionate and Luke seemingly falling in love with Polly because of it. She could see it on his face, this look of wonder that Polly knew exactly what she wanted to make her dreams come true. Flick wondered if that was the reason Luke wanted Polly to come and work there – because he'd had feelings for her all along. Although it was a bit late for him to do anything now, he was leaving in a few weeks.

It didn't matter. Let them have fun for a few weeks. If Polly could run the café half as well as she could run her catering van, then the café would be a big success and that was the only thing that did matter. And it wasn't like Flick had any claim over Luke, she'd known him for a day. Just because her silly, impulsive heart had started having feelings for him, it didn't mean anything. And this way was better because if anything did happen between her and Luke she could fall for him very easily and then he'd leave and she'd get her heart broken. So she would be happy for him and ignore the ache in her heart that said otherwise.

∼

Flick was sitting up on the roof terrace, looking out on the incredible view of the town. It was late and she'd spent hours coming up with ideas of how to help the studios and lost track of time so her dinner of a ham and cheese toastie was more like a late supper. Luke suddenly climbed up the steps to join her. He was wearing his glasses again tonight and there was something so sexy about them. She tried to push that thought away, she didn't need to be thinking things like that.

'Hey,' Flick said, offering out the triangles of ham and cheese toastie.

Luke picked one up and took a bite of the cheesy gooeyness. 'Mmm, thank you. I haven't had a chance to eat anything yet, it's been a busy day.'

'Yeah, sorry, I feel like you've picked up a lot of the workload.'

'We're a team, you can't do it all on your own. And I know tradesmen around here, a lot of them are friends so I can get some of the work done very quickly. In fact the painting will be done tomorrow. Well some of it, the flowers and bees will have to wait until I can get a mural artist, unless I can persuade Rose to paint them.'

Polly had decided to continue her bumblebee theme in the café with yellow walls painted with bees and flowers, just like her van. The tables were going to be black or some kind of iridescent resin to represent the bees' wings. It was going to look good when it was finished. And with the huge list of shiny new appliances that Polly had insisted she needed, it was going to be the best-stocked café in the town, possibly the world.

'I worry about you spending too much money on this. Polly's renovations and new equipment are going to cost thousands and I don't know how big this kitty is but it's not bottomless. I know you said you had some money in your savings, I worry you're subsidising this with your own money.'

Luke smiled. 'You really don't need to be worried.'

'Of course I do. If you're paying out for this, that's not fair.'

'Look, I know people, I can get a lot of the kitchen things cheap so you don't need to worry about the kitty running out of money.'

'How cheap, like fallen-off-the-back-of-a-lorry cheap?'

He laughed. 'One of my friends remodels kitchens for businesses: cafés, restaurants, hotels. When a company remodels their kitchen they have stuff they want to get rid of. They don't care what happens to it, as long as it's gone. My friend stores them, sometimes does them up if need be and sells them on.'

'OK, but some of the gadgets and machines Polly wants sound really fancy. She's not going to be happy with second-hand goods.'

'Let me worry about that.'

Flick scowled, not convinced that Luke knowing a few people was going to help with this. She didn't know a lot about kitchen equipment but she'd seen the prices of a few of the items Polly wanted and some of them were crazy expensive. The money had to be coming from somewhere.

'Maybe we should put a pin in the gift shop until the café is up and running. We can't just keep spending money with no money coming in and I don't want you or the kitty to be short.'

'We have to spend money to make money. The café will look great and people will come here to see it. As you said, getting people through the door is half the problem. If the artists don't want to capitalise on the extra footfall, then there's no helping them. And no, you're not backing out of the gift shop. That will be an attraction as well.'

'But where is the money coming from? I promised to look after the studios for my nan and I can't let her come back to find that we're fifty thousand pounds in debt. And let's face it, if she had that kind of money just lying around, she wouldn't be in such financial difficulty that she was thinking of selling the place.'

'There won't be any debt, I promise. Consider the kitty a gift from a fairy godmother.'

She narrowed her eyes. 'You see, fairy godmothers normally want something in return like your first-born child, or a pound of flesh.'

'That was *The Merchant of Venice*, and Shylock was not so much a cute, whimsical godmother with a magic wand and more a vengeful, greedy man obsessed with wealth, power and revenge.'

She smiled that of course he would know his Shakespeare. The books on his bookshelf were clearly not just there for show.

'I promise you that your first-born and all body parts are perfectly safe,' Luke said.

She looked at him and knew she could trust him, at least in that regard. He wasn't going to lead her down some dodgy rabbit hole with loan sharks or the mafia chasing them for money. And maybe she'd watched too many movies and was seeing shadows when there was only light. This was a good thing. They really couldn't save the studios without some kind of outlay. She just wished it wasn't quite so much.

'I just feel that if this is going to be my business, I need to contribute towards it, not freeload off the kitty. I don't have any money in my savings but I do have an antique sapphire necklace my aunt left me in her will. The sapphire is quite small but it's very pretty. I might get a hundred or so for that.' She bit her lip. 'I could sell my car.'

'There's no need to do that. The gift shop will benefit

the studios too so it's only right it's fully funded by the kitty.'

'I don't feel right about it.'

'Well, we can always work out some kind of repayment. A percentage of all sales goes back into the kitty. The rest, after paying you a wage, can go to buying more stock.'

'I'd feel better if I can repay something.'

'That's fine. We can sort something out that's fair but I don't want you to worry about this.'

She nodded, feeling a little bit better about it, and carried on eating her toastie.

'You still haven't told me why you aren't interested in Natalia or the other women in your fan club. Natalia is very pretty.'

'Oh… they're not my type.'

'Oh.' Flick chewed her lip for a moment as she prepared herself to rip off the sticking plaster. 'Is Polly your type?'

'Polly? No, she's nice, I think she'll be a great asset to the team over here but I haven't thought about her in that way. She's a bit young for me and I think she's probably just like the others in many ways.'

Flick didn't know what he meant by that; Polly and Natalia were nothing alike. She was also desperate to know if she was his type but she couldn't ask that. And what would be the point, she didn't want to start something with him when he was leaving. She'd never been the sort of person to just have a casual fling. She watched him sigh sadly about the unwanted attention from Natalia.

'You know, the easiest way to get Natalia, or any of the others who keep following you around, to leave you alone would be to tell them you have a girlfriend.'

'I don't think they'll believe it.'

'Why? You're a good-looking man, lovely, kind. Why is it so hard to believe you have a girlfriend?'

'I'm just not known for a successful romantic history. I'm a nerd. Nerds don't get the women.'

'That's not true. And you're not a nerd.'

'I have a million useless facts stored away in my brain, my career before wood carving was playing with computers. I'll watch nature programmes and find them fascinating, I have a telescope to look at the stars. You've seen the books I read, I could talk for hours about my love of Pratchett. At the pirate festival I will be going in full pirate regalia and I often go to comic cons dressed as Aragorn from *Lord of the Rings*.'

She smiled at that. None of that put her off, she found it all very endearing.

'And you've never found anyone to be your Arwen?' she asked, referring to Aragorn's soul mate.

'Never been that lucky.'

'Well, I could be your girlfriend.'

He stared at her. 'What?'

'We can pretend to be together.'

'Pretend. Right, yes, of course.'

'When Natalia comes up here, you tell her you have a girlfriend and we can pretend to be a loving couple.

She'll soon give up once she sees how happy and in love you are.'

'I'm not sure I'm comfortable with lying. Or be any good at it.'

'So you'd rather keep hiding in the cupboard every time she visits?'

'Well no.'

'And I take it you don't just want to tell her a firm no and to leave you alone?'

'No, I don't particularly like confrontation.'

'Don't you think this could be worth a go, just to get some peace and quiet?'

'I suppose.'

Luke looked really uncomfortable with the idea and Flick wondered if it wasn't just the idea of lying to people but the horror of having to pretend he was her boyfriend.

'Or just keep hiding in a cupboard, it's no skin off my nose. It was just a suggestion. I don't mind holding your hand and looking at you adoringly. But if you don't want to do that, I'm sure avoiding her will continue to work just as well. Or find the courage of Aragorn and tell her to sling her hook.'

'Will we kiss?' Luke asked.

Flick felt her eyebrows shoot up. She hadn't thought about that. 'Well, I guess we could, if you want, just to be completely convincing. It's just a kiss, it doesn't mean anything. It's not like you'll be making love to me in the middle of your studio just to show we're in love, but a kiss…' She shrugged to show it was nothing when all she could think about was how much she'd wanted that when they were standing in the secret cupboard earlier. This was turning out to be not quite so selfless as she'd first thought.

'OK, let's give it a go,' Luke said.

'The kiss?' Flick almost squeaked.

'No, us, together. At least the pretence of it.'

'OK,' Flick said, suddenly wondering if this wasn't such a great idea after all. Could she really kiss him and not feel anything at all?

'Right, I'm going to bed,' Luke said, standing up.

'Night, lover boy,' Flick teased.

He paused and even in the darkness she could see him blush.

'Night Flick,' he said, softly.

He disappeared down the ladder and Flick couldn't help smiling. This was going to be fun.

CHAPTER SIX

The painters and decorators arrived early the next day and were already hard at work. A lot of them Luke knew from the pub quiz team and, as it was only a quick paint job, they'd bumped him to the top of their list. They were busily transforming the café into something wonderful. The sunshine-yellow walls really brightened up the place and Rose had agreed to paint the bees and flowers once it was done in return for free coffee and cake for a month once the café was up and running.

Luke had spent the night before painstakingly going through Polly's list of everything she apparently needed to run the café and ordering the items online. Blenders, smoothie makers, ice cream makers, bread makers, waffle makers, pancake makers. There was a machine for everything, even things he had never thought of or heard of before. Polly had clearly been imagining her dream café for some time, creating her perfect wish-list of gadgets and must-have accessories, and when she found out who was footing the bill she decided not to hold back. And while he was happy to try and support people's dreams he was pretty sure the café didn't need self-heating butter knives for the customers or teapots that could brew two different kinds of tea simultaneously and he was fairly confident that no one in the world needed a strawberry stem remover. What was wrong with a knife? But while he was well aware he was being taken for a ride here, he was going to go ahead with it because he wanted the café to be a success, which in turn would help the studios back on its feet.

And this was exactly the kind of thing he was running away from. Over the past year, since everyone had found out who he was, he'd paid out for a new roof for someone after a tree had gone through it and the insurance company had refused to pay out, a new washing machine for a single mother of two, new tyres for a young family's car, a new oven for a local café, a newly decorated nursery with all the furniture for a couple expecting triplets, a new bike for a kid whose bike had been stolen, a new car, a new van, a new wheelbarrow, a new laptop, a new bed, a new dining room table, a new shed, the list was endless. And he didn't know any of these people who suddenly wanted to be his best friend. Then there were the big things he'd been coerced into buying: a new lifeboat for the town, new enclosures at the local dog shelter, a summerhouse at the local school. He was all for helping charities, he'd given millions to them over the years, but the constant expectation that he would always put his hand in his pocket and pay out was growing quite tiring. He was looking forward to walking the streets of Skye and having no one know who he was.

The only people never to ask for anything from him were Audrey and Quinn. In fact, Audrey was quite insistent that she never wanted his money, even when he offered.

And then there was Flick, worried about spending too much, wanting to pay him back, or rather the fictional kitty, out of her profits. No one had ever wanted to pay him back before. Granted, things might change once she knew how much money he had in his bank, just like everyone else who looked at him with pound signs in their eyes, but he liked her attitude, at least for now.

Although he knew it was more than that that he liked. She was kind and easy to talk to. She made him laugh.

He was useless with women, never knowing the right thing to say, always awkward, always worried that the women he was with were enjoying themselves. One of his ex-girlfriends had likened him to a puppy desperate for that pat on the head and to be told he was a good boy. Although rude, there was probably an element of truth in it. She'd laughed when he'd asked permission to kiss her and said women just liked to be grabbed and kissed, which didn't seem very polite or gentlemanly. She'd mocked him when they'd first made love because he'd asked her if she was OK and if she liked how he was touching her. She'd said real men went in all guns blazing, they didn't hold back. She'd laughed at his love of *The Lord of the Rings* and ridiculed him when she found out he liked to dress up as Aragorn for comic cons. Consequently he'd always been a bit withdrawn around women, never showing his true self. And if he was honest, a bit of a bumbling twat.

But Flick genuinely seemed to like him, he felt like he could truly be himself with her and she wouldn't judge him or laugh at him. Even if they would only ever be friends. He had to admit, his heart had leapt with happiness when she said she wanted to be his girlfriend and then flopped with disappointment when he realised it would only be pretend. Although she had seemed quite open to the idea of a kiss, maybe even a little bit excited. Was it possible that she was looking forward to the kiss as much as he was? Or was he seeing something that simply wasn't there?

Promising the boys he'd get them pizza for lunch, he went back downstairs to his studio space and carried on working on some of the smaller wooden animals he was making to sell in his studio. He was actually really enjoying working on the smaller pieces, although he did feel there was probably more attention to detail needed at this size than less.

He wasn't sure if the other studio owners had decided to create smaller or cheaper items. He knew Katherine had started creating smaller mosaics but he had no idea what the intentions of the other artists were.

Just then Flick appeared in his doorway and he tried to ignore how his heart leapt when she smiled at him.

'Hey,' she said, coming in.

He loved the clothes she wore, little dresses with dogs or cats or guinea pigs on them. Today's dress sported turtles swimming through the coral with little fishes darting around them. She moved closer and the sweet smell of coconut and mango washed over him. He shook his head to clear it. Why was he noticing stuff like that? After walking in on him naked, she was never going to look at him in any way other than as a friend and with him leaving he shouldn't want her to want anything more than that.

'These look great.' Flick picked up a small wooden owl and he felt a small surge of pride. 'They look really intricate.'

'Yeah, turns out I can't really do something simple.'

'How long did it take you?'

'That one, about two or three hours. But I really enjoyed it. The big stag over there has taken weeks, so it's nice to have something finished in such a short time. I figured I can spend two days a week making these smaller items over the next few weeks and the other five on commissions.'

'Do you not take a day off?'

'I do if I have something else to do, if I'm going out or meeting someone. Being my own boss is flexible, I can work whenever I want. But I love doing this, so it doesn't feel like a job for me. Doing it seven days a week isn't a chore.'

'That's true. I love making my wish jars. Even after I've been at work all day, it feels like a reward to be able to spend time doing that in the evening.'

He noticed the tablet in her hand. 'Have you completed your shopping list?'

'Yes, but there's quite a bit. If you wanted to put a cap on it and stop buying things when I reach that cap, that's fine.'

'No, we want to go big with our grand reopening, new café, new gift shop, we want people to be wowed when they come up here.'

'Ooh, we should do a proper grand reopening, invite people up here for cake or cocktails or champagne.'

'Three important food groups right there.'

She laughed and he loved that he could have that effect on her.

She handed him the tablet and pointed out the two different internet tabs. 'This one is all the gifts: the scarves, mugs, candles, etc. This one is all the craft paraphernalia so people can have a go at creating their own masterpieces after walking around and seeing all the ones here in the studios.'

'Perfect, I'll get everything ordered today.'

She bit her lip. 'I would feel better if I knew where all this money was coming from.'

'I told you, we have a kitty.'

'Luke.'

He sighed, knowing she wasn't going to let this go. 'OK, OK, we have an anonymous donor.'

'Who?'

Of course she would want to know who. 'That's the beauty of being anonymous, no one knows.'

'But *you* know, this money didn't just magically appear.'

'Yes *I* know, but I can't say anything more than that. I promised them complete anonymity.'

'Does my nan know who they are?'

He pulled a face, wishing he'd never mentioned the anonymous donor. 'I think if you asked her she would probably know but I think you should respect the donor's wishes to remain anonymous and not try to find out.'

She frowned in confusion. 'OK, but why have they donated?'

'Because… they believe in the place and the importance of its legacy. They obviously knew the place was in trouble and wanted to help.'

'But my nan didn't tell any of the artists, not even you, how much trouble she was in. So why was she sharing it with this random donor?'

'I don't know. '"Ours is not to reason why."'

She sighed, clearly not impressed with him quoting Tennyson. And he didn't blame her, if he was in her shoes, he'd want answers too. He wondered if she would be more or less impressed if he quoted Sir Walter Scott. "Oh, what a tangled web we weave, when first we practise to deceive." Probably less, a lot less.

'OK,' she nodded thoughtfully. 'If this donor believes in this place so much that they want to donate money for its upkeep, then we need to give them something impressive, something wonderful for their money. But will you let them know, that for my part, I will repay them? It might take some time, but I will.'

'You really don't need to worry, but if it makes you feel better then you can repay the kitty as and when you can. But there's no rush. Focus your attention and your profits into making the gift shop a success. Worry about the kitty later.'

She nodded although Luke could see she wasn't happy about it.

'Have you spoken to any of the other artists, about whether they are staying or going?' Flick asked.

'No, Ethel glared at me this morning when I walked past her studio so I didn't dare. I'm sure she thinks I'm sleeping with the enemy… erm, in the non-literal sense.'

Flick laughed. 'Well, us pretending to be together isn't going to quell those thoughts.'

Luke shrugged. 'Let them talk. Besides, if you're the enemy for trying to help them I'd rather be on your side any day. Some people are not worth saving and it's the studios that matters, not them. If they walk, we'll find new artists. There's so many in Lovegrove Bay.'

'Yeah, you're right,' Flick said, sadly. 'I just hate the thought of kicking anyone out. My grandad would never have done that, but then he had a way of talking that people listened to. I think it was the importance of what he was doing here, people believed in it.'

'Then we need to get them to believe in it again.'

Luke heard a car door close outside and he looked

out the window to see Natalia walking up the drive towards the front door.

His heart sank. Not again. She was relentless in her pursuit of him and he wasn't stupid enough to believe this was motivated by anything but money.

'Natalia's coming,' Luke said, wondering if it wasn't too late to run and hide.

'Quick, put your arm around me,' Flick said.

He did as he was told, slinging an arm around her shoulders.

'Not like that, it's too brotherly.'

'I could hold your hand instead,' he said, slipping his hand into hers and trying not to like it so much.

'Yes, that works, although we've not had a chance to come up with our story yet.'

'We need a story?' Luke asked in alarm, looking out the window to see they only had a few seconds left.

'Yes, where we met, how long we've been dating, what's my favourite colour.'

'She isn't going to ask that.'

'Maybe not but we have to be convincing. Right now, we're just two people holding hands. Correction, one woman, one rabbit in the headlights.'

'Well, what should we do?'

She leaned up and kissed him.

He heard himself gasp against her mouth in surprise. They'd talked about this but he hadn't expected it to happen so quickly and without any warning. But then he wrapped his arms around her and kissed her back and it wasn't because Natalia was coming in, it was because she tasted so damned good, because when her mouth met his he felt a kick of desire and need slam into his stomach. She slid her hands round the back of his neck, stroking his hair, and he groaned softly against her lips at the sensation of it. He relished the feel of her warm body tight against his. The outside world faded away, he forgot about Natalia or saving the studios, he could only focus on how perfectly she fitted in his arms, how her soft lips felt against his, her incredible scent, and how this might be the best damn kiss of his life.

He moved his hands up her back, touching her bare flesh on her shoulders which made her moan softly.

He pulled back a fraction to look at her and could feel her breath was heavy on his lips. He could see her eyes were dark with… something. He didn't want to attribute that to lust or passion or desire, just because that was what he was feeling. But they were dark and she was looking at him in complete wonder.

He had no idea if Natalia had come and gone or whether she was still there and he didn't care. He cupped Flick's face and kissed her again and felt her melt against him, her fingers tightening in his t-shirt. He had never felt so turned on from a simple kiss before and he suddenly wanted nothing more than to scoop her up, carry her up to his room and make love to her. And with the way she was kissing him so passionately, it seemed she wanted that too. This kiss was everything but he suddenly remembered that actually it was nothing. It was an act, nothing more, and he'd completely lost his mind.

He pulled back and was just about to apologise for taking it too far when he realised they weren't alone in the room. He looked up expecting to see Natalia but she was nowhere to be seen. Instead Ethel was standing there watching them, her mouth hanging open.

She cleared her throat. 'Well this is a surprise.'

Flick took his hand. 'For us too.'

Luke looked down at her and she smiled up at him happily. Either she was playing the part really well or she had somehow completely fallen in love with him over the last few minutes. He sighed, softly. He was a fool if he thought it was the latter.

'Well, now we know why you're fighting her corner so hard,' Ethel said.

'I'm fighting her corner because it's the right thing to do. Unless we change we'll lose this place forever.'

'Well, I actually came down to tell Flick that I won't be taking part. I won't be producing cheap tat for the tourists, that's not who I am. I'm very happy here and I'll be sad to go but I'm not lowering myself to that.'

Luke felt Flick visibly deflate next to him. 'Oh, I, erm… It's such a shame you feel this way. Is there anything we can do to change your mind?'

'No. I'm an excellent quilter. I won best quilter in the south-west six years in a row and two years ago I won best quilter in England. When people buy quilts from me, they are buying quilts from an award-winning, professional quilter and that comes with a price tag.'

'No one is doubting your credentials,' Flick said, weirdly still holding Luke's hand. 'Your quilts are probably the most beautiful quilts I've ever seen in my life. The attention to detail, the exquisite embroidery, it's incredible. I have no doubt at all that they are worth the high price tag. But the problem is, right now, no one is buying them. Unless you're selling them online or somewhere else I don't know about, you haven't made a single sale in six months. Or more. You have hundreds of them in your studio, all stacked up in piles. And yes, the complete lack of footfall is a big part of that but when we open the café and the gift shop that will bring people here, we have to give them something to buy. Ninety-nine percent of the people who will walk through those doors will not have three thousand pounds to spend on a piece of art. And I don't want you to produce tat. You could embroider and frame small pictures of animals. Baby animals are very popular decorations for nurseries. It could still be your high-quality embroidery but on a much smaller scale.'

'How small?' Ethel said.

'Six inches?' Flick tried.

Ethel didn't say anything and Luke could see she was wavering.

'Why don't we display your award-winning quilts on the walls and I'll take photos of the rest and we can project them onto the walls in a kind of slideshow?' Luke quickly offered. 'We can carefully pack away the rest in storage and display some of your embroidery pieces instead.'

Ethel sighed. 'I did enjoy creating some embroidery

pictures of baby Australian animals when my great-niece had a baby.'

'Couldn't we at least get you to try embroidering some animal pictures and see if it's something you would like to do long term? You can still do your quilts as well,' Flick said.

'How about a deal?' Ethel said. 'If I sell one of my quilts at full price within one month of the café reopening, you'll leave me be to continue making them?'

'OK,' Flick said, cautiously. 'But we will have to reassess in six months' time. One a month is fine, but one a year is not feasible.'

Ethel nodded her head to concede this. 'But in the meantime I will make twenty embroidered animal pictures and we'll see how well they sell in the first month too.'

'They have to be less than thirty pounds,' Flick reminded her.

Ethel scowled but nodded. 'Very well. We'll give it one month.'

With that, she walked out. Flick still continued to hold Luke's hand even when there was no one there to see it, making his heart do weird things in his chest.

'Well, that was a success,' Flick said.

'The kiss or our conversation with Ethel?'

She grinned at him. 'Oh, the kiss was very successful. I wasn't expecting the hottest kiss of my life.'

'I am sorry.'

She looked at him in surprise. 'For what?'

'Well, I know we talked about kissing but I got a bit

carried away and it turned into something a bit more… pornographic. I'm sorry, that's not what you signed up for when you agreed to help me.'

She frowned in confusion. 'You're… You're apologising for kissing me with passion and desire?'

'Well, it wasn't real, was it?'

Her face fell. She let go of his hand and took a step back and then another. 'No, of course not. It meant nothing, obviously.' She took another step back. 'I just meant it was successful because it clearly sent Natalia packing. We were very convincing. We do that a few more times and your fan club will get the message.' She started walking towards the door. 'And thanks for your help with Ethel.'

'Flick…'

'I should go, I, umm… I'm going into the town to speak to some of the artists at the local outdoor market.'

'I could come with you.'

'No. No need. See you later.'

She made her way out through the main front door and he watched her shoulders slump as she walked down the drive.

Why did he feel like such a twat?

∾

Flick walked down the hill towards the pretty little harbour, with its little white boats bobbing around in a warm summer breeze. The shops and cafés were clustered around the outside of the harbour on the main road, all painted in bright colours. Everything looked so cute and charming in the sunshine. There was a shop selling ice creams of every flavour, a shop selling beach paraphernalia like towels, sun hats and Crocs and everything in between. There was a shop selling beach-themed accessories for the home, lighthouses, driftwood trees, decorations made from sea glass. And yes, some may argue it was tat for the tourists, but Flick always loved looking at the different ornaments that people had made. There were other shops here too. An old vintage record shop that also sold vintage t-shirts and photos. There was a bookshop, a florist and the biggest costume shop she'd ever seen, hiring out everything from dinosaurs to Batman costumes.

She walked past the harbour and down the steps onto Blossom Beach. She slipped off her sandals and walked across the warm, white sand barefooted until she reached the sea.

She felt like such an idiot. When she'd suggested the stupid idea of pretending to be Luke's girlfriend to scare off his fan club, he'd been the one to ask if they would kiss. And as she lay in bed last night, thinking it through, she'd begun to wonder, or even hope that Luke had asked that because he wanted to kiss her, because she hadn't imagined that moment they'd shared together in the cupboard. And then something had happened when she had kissed Luke, they had shared a connection that went way beyond a simple kiss. He had kissed her with so much passion and adoration that she'd thought for one stupid moment that it had been real and that he liked her as much as she liked him. But it had all been fake, just a meaningless kiss. She was surprised by how much that hurt when she'd known that was all it was before she'd kissed him.

Just then her phone rang. She fished it out of her pocket and smiled to see it was her friend Tabitha. She quickly answered it.

'Hey gorgeous, how you doing?' Tabitha asked.

Flick sighed. 'Well, all the artists working at the house hate me because they don't like change, some of them are threatening to leave and if they all do I'll have no one left to save the studios for, I've somehow agreed to run the gift shop with no business skills or experience and I may just have developed a rather annoying and completely inappropriate crush on my flatmate and colleague.'

Tabitha laughed. 'That's a lot to unpack.'

'It really is.'

'OK, first off, when you were telling me about Waterfall House and how you were going off to save it, you were telling me all about the therapeutic art workshops your grandad ran and how important that was to you and to everyone involved.'

'Yeah, it was. It *is*, but we've not run the workshops here since he died. It's just the artists now creating their products and trying, very unsuccessfully, to sell them.'

'Far be it for me to tell you how to run the place. I can't even run my own home – you've seen the state of my house.'

'You have three kids, two of them twin boys under

the age of three, plus a whole menagerie of animals. I think you can be excused if your house is a little messy.'

'Anyway, the point is, you have to give them something to fight for. Right now, they're just muddling along, creating their art and it doesn't matter if no one buys it because they clearly don't need the money or they'd have done something about the lack of sales before now. The whole reason why your grandad bought the house was because he wanted to offer art to people who'd had brain injuries – a cause very close to my heart as you're aware. That's the legacy you should be saving, not just the studio space for the artists. Your dream of being able to have a shop selling everything people need to create their own works of art is because you recognise the importance of art and being creative and how everyone should have that opportunity, not just the five artists who work there. Also why would you want to bust your ass to save the place for them when they seem very ungrateful about the help you're offering them?'

'Are you suggesting I bring back the workshops?'

'That's exactly what I'm saying. Ask the artists who have studios there to run one specific to their art. Ask art teachers to do them. You do it in the name of Headway or Brainwave, both excellent brain injury charities in the UK, and if you choose to charge for the workshops you could give twenty-five percent of the profits to one of those charities. I bet you'll have lots of people who will want to help and it brings awareness to those charities too. It will inspire the artists who work there to do something to help save the studios because it's not just them anymore, it's the workshops and the people who use them. You can even do workshops for people who don't have injuries as studies have shown how important art is for mental health too. Make your studios for everyone.'

'Tabitha, that's an excellent idea. I've been so caught up in saving the studios for my grandad, but you're right. It's his legacy that I should be saving, not the artists. And the workshops will make them care again. Honestly, I could kiss you.'

'Well save those kisses for your man, let's talk about him.'

Flick felt her heart sink again after having her hopes lifted with talk of the workshops. She was going to have to face Luke again at some point and probably have an honest conversation with him.

'Luke is lovely, sweet, kind and funny and I really like him. Well, more than like him if I'm honest. We share a connection that's...' She paused as she tried to describe how he made her feel, how she felt drawn to him, how just being around him made her smile so damn much. 'It's not something I've felt before. It's something special, well it is for me. Frustratingly, he's also moving to Scotland in a few weeks so there really isn't any point in starting something. But I agreed to pretend to be his girlfriend to get rid of some women who won't take no for an answer and keep following him around.'

'That sounds very selfless,' Tabitha laughed.

'Well, the suggestion probably was. I just thought we'd hold hands and look adoringly at each other. But then he asked if we would kiss as part of the pretence and I realised I wanted that a lot more than I should as a friend doing him a favour, so not altruistic at all as it turns out. Anyway, this woman who won't leave him alone just turned up and we kissed.'

Flick touched her lips, remembering how it felt, remembering the feeling of being held in his arms, as if they fitted together so perfectly. 'And I enjoyed it a bit too much and I thought he did too. He was so… passionate and Christ, Tabby, it was probably the best kiss of my life and I've had quite a few passionate kisses in my time. But afterwards, he completely back-pedalled away from it. Apologised for taking the charade too far and then basically said, oh obviously it's not real. He wanted to make sure I knew it wasn't real, that it meant nothing to him.'

Her cheeks flamed with mortification. 'And now I feel really embarrassed. I moaned. Who moans from a simple kiss? But he was turning me on so much just from his kiss and I moaned when he touched my bare shoulder, because I really wanted him to touch all over my body. If he'd scooped me up in his arms and carried me off to his bed, there wasn't a single part of me that didn't want that. In fact, I was probably five seconds away from taking him by the hand and taking him to bed myself. How sad and desperate is that? I've never felt like that before, with any man. And now I'm sure he knows how much I wanted him and I'd quite like to run away and hide and never face him again.'

Tabitha laughed. 'Oh honey, unfortunately you can't do that, you have an art studio to save. But he must be someone really amazing if you're considering breaking your no sex ban.'

Flick pulled a face. 'There was never an official ban in place, I just haven't fancied it for a few years.'

'Because of Red Flag Ryan.'

'Well yes, he kind of put me off.'

'But you've dated other people since Ryan and you didn't want sex from them either. Why is Luke different?'

'Because I trust him.' She was surprised that answer came so easily and actually how important that was to her. She'd only known him a few days. It would normally take weeks to build enough trust to want to go to bed with someone and, as it turned out, she'd never got there with the last few men she'd dated. But with Luke she just knew she could trust him completely.

'Oh honey. I think next time you see him just laugh it off if he brings it up. Tell him you did amateur dramatics and you can be really convincing when you need to be. But honestly, if he was kissing you passionately and then apologised for taking it too far, it sounds like he was enjoying himself a bit too much too and was then embarrassed in case you laughed it off so he got in there first.'

Flick bit her lip. 'Do you think?'

'I think you can tell when a kiss is real. I know you

have a long history of dating disasters and some of them have been complete arseholes so you don't have a lot of good men to compare this to but there's a big difference between a fake kiss and a real one.'

'Have you had many fake kisses?' Flick asked.

'Have I had many kisses where I didn't care for the man and they didn't care for me? Lots. There's a huge difference when someone does really care for you or want to be with you. You can feel it.'

'Well, that's what I thought. There was clearly a mutual attraction when we kissed, but when he tried to dismiss it I thought maybe it was all one-sided and I was just seeing what I wanted to see.'

'Maybe you should have a chat with him.'

'Urgh, maybe not. He's already got a load of women throwing their unwanted advances at him, he doesn't need another.'

Flick couldn't think of anything worse than Luke hiding himself in a cupboard every time he saw her.

'Well, will there be more fake kisses?' Tabitha asked.

Flick hadn't thought about that. 'I suppose there might be.'

'Then I'll guess you'll find out then.'

Flick sighed, not wanting to think about the embarrassment of another fake kiss and trying to keep her heart and body firmly detached from it. 'I don't think it matters whether it's fake or real anyway, he's moving to Scotland in just a few weeks. That's not exactly a great start to a relationship.'

'It's Scotland, not the other side of the world. And

people have had very successful long-distance relationships much further away than that. He sounds like he's someone special so if the kisses turn out to be real or turn into something more, don't shy away from it just because he's moving. Enjoy it, embrace it, see if you have something worth pursuing. And if nothing else you can have fun putting the ghost of Ryan to bed once and for all. You deserve to have some fun with someone lovely.'

Flick thought about what it would be like to have a fling with someone as wonderful as Luke, someone she could trust. If he made love half as passionately as he kissed, it would be utterly magnificent. She shook her head. Why was she thinking like that? He'd practically pushed her away after the kiss. Unless he'd done that because he knew he was moving and didn't want to get involved with her when he was leaving in a few weeks.

Why was she second-guessing everything? She didn't need any complications right now, she had a studio to save. She decided to change the subject.

'How are you anyway?'

'Oh, we've stupidly decided to breed the pigs and Harmony is due to pop any day now. The cat we rescued two weeks ago, Nigel, turned out to be Nigella and she's just given birth to seven little kittens. The stick insects are reproducing faster than I change my underwear – every time I blink, there's another baby in the tank. Cora is very excited about all the babies and potential babies, let me tell you. The twins just want to grab everything so I'm having to keep them and the cats and the twiglets apart. Honestly, I think I might have to open a zoo soon. The twins' toilet training is not going well, they love their poo. They keep sneaking off and pooing everywhere that isn't the toilet and think the whole thing is hilarious.'

Flick smiled. 'You secretly love your life.'

'I think I'd rather be fighting to save an art studio and having hot kisses with sexy men right now.'

'Hey,' came the indignant voice of Dave, Tabitha's lovely husband, in the background.

'Oh, you know I love you really. I'll have to live vicariously through you, Flick. Keep me posted.'

They said their goodbyes and Tabitha hung up. Flick would rather be dealing with baby stick insects, or twiglets as Tabitha called them, than grumpy artists and facing Luke Donnelly after that kiss.

CHAPTER SEVEN

Luke had just started carving a small flamingo when the front door opened. He looked up hoping to see Flick but his heart dropped when Natalia walked in. Luke debated whether he still had time to run out of the studio and hide but decided that was probably too rude. Besides, as Flick suggested, maybe it was time he dug deep and found some of that courage that Aragorn was so famous for.

He hadn't had too many conversations with Natalia and had successfully managed to avoid her for the last few months. But every conversation he'd had, no matter how brief he'd managed to keep it, always revolved around sex. The first time they'd met in a pub, she introduced herself, told him to buy her a drink which he had, not because he was attracted to her but because he always had a hard time saying no. Then without any preamble or small talk, she pulled her phone out of her pocket, showed him a photo of an eight-thousand-pound ruby necklace and told him if he bought that for her, she would have sex with him wearing it. He'd made his excuses and got out of there as fast as he could.

But she hadn't given up. Every time she saw him she'd offer him an amazing night of sex, in return for something flashy and expensive she wanted him to buy her. At least her terms and conditions were clear. And she was consistent, he'd give her that. He wasn't expecting this conversation to be any different.

'I saw you with your little girlfriend earlier. I can't help thinking you were doing that to make me jealous,' Natalia said, walking towards him.

Her ego was clearly so big, nothing could dent it.

'Why would I try to make you jealous?'

'Because you're playing hard to get.'

'Is that what you think I'm doing?'

'Well of course. I can get any man I want. These breasts are real, you know.'

He felt his eyes widen in shock. He stopped himself from saying that he didn't care.

'You can check for yourself.' She moved within touching distance and he took a large step back.

'No, I absolutely do not want to touch your breasts.'

'Of course you do. Every man wants to touch my breasts. Men have had whole conversations with my breasts instead of looking me in the eye.'

There was something really sad about that.

'No man has ever turned me down before. You have no idea what you're missing, I'd be the best sex you'll ever have.'

Luke tried not to pull a face but this whole conversation was making him cringe.

'Is that what this is about? There was me thinking it was just about my money, but it's your pride, isn't it? You can't believe I said no.'

She scowled at him. 'No, it's definitely about your money. Let's face it, you don't have anything else going for you.'

'Oh, so now you think being rude to me will seal the deal.'

She sighed, clearly seeing the emerald necklace or diamond earrings she so desperately wanted slipping between her fingers. 'What has she got that I don't have? From what I could see, she wasn't even very pretty.'

He smiled. 'She's the most beautiful woman I've met, inside and out. She's kind, generous, funny and she likes me for me, not my money.'

'Oh, don't talk crap. Of course she's with you for your money.'

'She has no idea I have any.'

She gave a spiteful little smile. 'But that's not true. I heard her in town the other day talking to someone. She said she had you exactly where she wanted you. She'd fooled you into believing she didn't know you were rich, got you to fall in love with her and now she was going to take you for every penny you had. That's why I came up here to warn you.'

He stared at her, not believing a word of it. Not least because their love story was a sham so Flick would hardly be boasting that she'd got him to fall in love with her, but mainly because she was the most genuine person he'd ever met. There was nothing fake or deceitful about her. He trusted her completely.

'When was this?'

'I don't know. Friday.'

'She didn't arrive until Saturday night.'

'And you two are kissing already, doesn't that show you what a gold digger she is?'

He raised his hand to stop her talking. 'Natalia, she makes me happy, very happy. And I've not had that for a very long time. This, between me and you, it's never going to happen, even if Flick hadn't come into my life like a... firework of joy, it still was never going to happen. Let it go.'

She huffed and then stormed out.

He watched her get back in her car and drive off and he felt inordinately proud of himself.

∼

Flick followed the beach round to the far side where there were steps up to the village green and where the outdoor craft market was. She bought a little pot of ice-cold mango sorbet on the way in and then started wandering round the stalls. A lot of them had pirate-themed items they were selling ahead of the pirate festival this Saturday but there was certainly an eclectic mix of different crafts available. There were chocolates, candles, soaps and perfumes. There were jewellery, paintings, clay, fused glass, stained glass, pictures made from twigs and leaves, animals made from needlefelt, crocheted animals, knitted animals, even animals or monsters made from forks and spoons. She wanted an artist who offered something unique, not only unique to the studios but unique within their own field or medium. She didn't want another painter, for example, unless it was completely different to what Rose offered.

She stopped at one stall that had tiny little sculptures made from the pages of books. They were so beautiful and intricate, little houses with their washing hanging on a line, a village pond with tiny paper ducks, a fairy-tale castle, a lighthouse, a forest scene, trees, flowers, various animals. They were stunning.

The woman carefully making a paper flower looked up at Flick and smiled.

'Hello, these are beautiful,' Flick said.

'Thank you.'

'I'm Felicity Hunter. Everyone calls me Flick.'

'Hi Flick, I'm Alex.'

'I'm from Waterfall House.' But when Alex looked at her blankly, Flick gestured to the house on the hill which seemed to preside over the whole town. 'The House with the Wonky Tree. We have several artists up there right now who make and sell their works of arts in their own studio space, but we also have quite a bit of unused space and we're looking for new artists to fill them.'

'Oh, you mean full time?'

'Yes.'

'Oh. I have a daughter. I have to take her and pick

her up from school, I'm not sure I'd have time to run my own studio.'

'You can fit it in around school hours and you can always bring your daughter back to the studios after school. But at least you'd have somewhere more permanent to make and sell your stuff. Somewhere that's just yours.'

Alex bit her lip. 'How much is the rent?'

'No rent, no bills, but we take twenty-five percent of all your profits.'

'That's quite a lot.'

'I've done craft markets myself and I know how much you probably paid for this table today. Some days I barely sold enough to break even.'

'Yeah, I've had days like that,' Alex agreed.

'This way the risk is all ours. On slow days when you don't get a sale, at least you haven't forked out for the cost of a table. And when you do get a sale, twenty-five percent will go towards the cost of our overheads. We're really not looking to make a profit from you, we just want to have enough to keep the studios from falling into debt.'

Alex nodded. 'I'll have to think about it.'

'Of course. Why don't you come up to the studios today, once you've finished here, and we can show you around?'

'OK, I will.'

'We have some provisos. Although it's great to have things like this on display in the showroom,' Flick gestured to a fairytale castle under a large glass dome that was at least two-foot high and a foot wide. 'We'd be looking for at least half your stock to be under thirty pounds. So smallish items that will appeal to the average person.'

'That's not a problem, most of these are between ten and twenty pounds,' Alex pointed to the smaller ones in jars at the front of her table. 'The castle is purely there to encourage commissions. Are there any other provisos?'

'Yes, sort of. We want to offer art workshops as that was the reason why the studios were opened in the first place. Originally the workshops were available to people who have suffered brain injuries, either from strokes or some other kind of trauma like a car accident, and we want to honour that legacy by doing the same. Eventually, we'll probably extend that to encompass workshops for everyone. Is that something you'd be willing to offer?'

'Yes absolutely. I'd be happy to help if you think this kind of thing is suitable.'

'Yes, I presume so. I'll be speaking to some of the brain injury charities to get advice on starting this thing, but what I gather from when my grandad did it, it's really no different to running any kind of art workshop. It's just about giving those with brain injuries the opportunity to do it with like-minded people and to make it as accessible as possible.'

'Sounds great. Even if I don't go ahead with moving into the studios, I'd still be happy to help with the workshops. My sister had brain trauma when she was thrown off her horse. On the surface she was absolutely fine, a few bruises and cuts, but it was simple things like buttoning up her shirt that she'd forgotten how to do or how to tie up her shoelaces. It took a while for her to learn how to do these things again.'

'I'm so sorry your sister went through that. My best friend went through something similar after a car accident. What you're talking about is called neuroplasticity, it's when the brain can find a route around the damage to be able to relay those messages on how to tie your shoelaces again, and things like art and crafts can really help with that.'

'Yes, absolutely, and I'd like to help with that.'

'OK, well we'll see you later this afternoon.'

'Yes, I'll be there around two thirty, as soon as I've finished here.'

Flick nodded and gave her a wave. She moved on to the other tables, admiring the work, and found a table selling jewel-decorated eggs and one selling beautiful paper quilling pictures. She repeated her spiel to them before doubling back to offer the same thing to the person who made monsters and animals out of forks and spoons because she really liked them and they were art even if people like Rose or Ethel might disapprove.

But when she got there she realised Quinn was the person making them.

'Hello again,' Flick said.

Quinn looked up and smiled at seeing her. 'Hello, how are you settling in?'

She thought about everything that had happened

since she walked through the doors of Waterfall House, that incredible kiss uppermost in her mind, and she tried hard not to blush as she remembered how her body had responded to Luke's touch.

'Oh fine,' she said, vaguely.

But clearly not vaguely enough as Quinn's face lit up. 'Fine?' he said, waggling his eyebrows, clearly bubbling with excitement.

She flushed with embarrassment; he obviously knew. 'Has he told you?'

'Told me what?' Quinn said, the monster he'd been working on clearly forgotten.

'About the kiss. Did he phone you as soon as I left or something?'

'I haven't spoken to him since yesterday. But now I want to know about the kiss.'

'Shit, you didn't know? But what was with all the eyebrow waggling?'

'Because the way you said fine was clearly, most definitely not fine.'

She cursed under her breath.

'So now I need to know all the details.'

'There's nothing to tell. It was a fake kiss.'

'A fake kiss?'

'Because Natalia won't leave him alone and I suggested we pretend to be together to get rid of her and we kissed and…' she trailed off.

Quinn smiled gently with understanding. 'And the kiss was a lot more than fake and now the two of you are second-guessing everything and wondering if the other felt it too?'

She sighed. 'Something like that. Well for my part.'

'I don't presume to know what you or Luke are feeling but I think trusting your heart is probably a good place to start.'

Flick decided to change the subject as it didn't seem right discussing this with Quinn when she hadn't discussed it with Luke.

'I'm on the hunt for new artists who might want to join us up on Waterfall Hill and I think you have exactly what we're looking for.'

She gave him her spiel and he listened but didn't ask the same questions that the others had asked. 'Who else have you spoken to about this?'

'So far, Suki who does the paper quilling pictures, Max who does the jewelled eggs and Alex who does the paper sculptures. They're all coming to have a look this afternoon.'

'Well I think I better come and look too. If nothing else, I might need to keep an eye on you two love birds.'

'I'm regretting inviting you now.'

'Why, I'll be in your corner.'

'What about Luke?'

'Depends if he's in your corner too.'

~

Luke was just finishing off the small flamingo when Flick came rushing back in with a big smile on her face.

'I know what we need to do to,' Flick said and he

couldn't help smiling at her enthusiasm. 'We need to start doing the workshops again, helping those whose lives have been impacted by brain injuries. That's why my grandad opened these studios in the first place, that's what he was passionate about and what the artists who worked here were passionate about too. That's what our anonymous donor cared about too, enough for him or her to donate thousands of pounds. We need to give the artists something to fight for, something to care about. That's the legacy I came here to save, not the artists' studios, especially when they don't really care about saving it themselves. So I'm going to ask them to teach workshops so they can be part of the change.'

'Yes! I love this idea,' Luke said. 'Partly that was the reason I wanted to come and work here so I could help people in the same way your grandad helped my mum. I was a bit disappointed to find the workshops didn't run anymore.'

'So will you help, will you be happy to teach, before you go anyway?'

'Yes, but I don't feel like I know enough about how to help people with brain injuries. Don't I need special training?'

'No, not with therapeutic art. I just spoke with someone from a local brain injury charity about this on the way back up here. They love that we're going to be offering this and they said they'd be happy to do a video conference call with the artists to talk through how to make their workshops accessible but they gave me some advice. They said art therapy is delivered by a specially trained art therapist but with therapeutic art it's about giving them the opportunities to maybe try something they've not tried before, teaching them a new skill, letting them express themselves, building their confidence, letting them use tools they might not have used before. You will have to be patient, explain things simply and not overload them with multiple instructions all at once. You may have to demonstrate it or explain it multiple times because those with some injuries will forget it very easily, but really it's just about being calm, quiet and friendly. You have nothing to worry about there, you're so lovely and kind and laid-back, this kind of thing is perfect for you.'

He felt warm inside at those words. It had been a long time since someone had seen past his bank balance and liked him for who he was. God, he really liked her and this passion and excitement for helping other people made him fall for her a little bit more. He really hoped he hadn't screwed things up with the kiss earlier when he'd wanted so much more. But he'd been so stunned by how heated the kiss was and how she had behaved towards him after because Flick having feelings for him too hadn't been on his radar. He'd wanted to make sure they were still on the same page, whether this was all still fake or whether she'd wanted more too. But it had sounded like he was dismissing it when he'd asked her if it was real and knew he'd hurt her in the process. And he was leaving in a few weeks, it felt silly to start something with her now but he knew he would always regret it if he didn't take this chance with her. He wanted to talk to her about it, take a risk and tell her his feelings, but he wasn't sure if now was the right time. Maybe tonight, over dinner.

He cleared his throat and refocussed on what she was saying. The workshops were important and he felt honoured she would trust him with them. 'Thank you. I'd be very happy to do it.'

'I've also potentially found four more artists who are going to come up to have a look and see if they're happy to move in. I've told them our terms and that some of their items need to be priced at less than thirty pounds so we'll see if they're willing to join our ranks. But I was chatting to Alex, she makes these sculptures like forests and seaside villages made from book pages. Anyway, her sister had brain trauma and Alex is very keen to help with the workshops even if she decides not to come up here as an artist so that will be good. And Quinn says he's going to come up and have a look to see if it suits him too.'

'Oh, it'll be good to have him up here. He's very laid-back and happy.'

Flick looked like she wanted to say something really uncomfortable. 'He knows about our kiss.'

'Oh?' He wasn't sure what to make of the fact that she was telling people. Was that good or bad?

'He said something which made me think he knew, I thought you'd phoned him to tell him and so I mentioned it. But I told him it was fake so you don't need to worry.'

'Right.'

That was definitely going to make for an awkward conversation with Quinn. He wouldn't let Luke hear the last of it.

'Anyway, I'm going to tell the other artists about the workshops. Let's hope they're as excited as I am about it. Or even a fraction excited. I'll take that.'

She turned to hurry out.

'Flick.'

She turned back.

'Are we good?'

Her cheeks flushed although he wasn't sure why. 'Oh yeah, we're fine,' she dismissed it with a wave and hurried out before he could say anything else to her.

∼

Flick let herself back into the flat later that night. She'd spent the afternoon showing the four new potential artists around the studios and talking to them about what she wanted to achieve at the studios. Alex and Quinn had agreed to come and join them. Max, the man who did the jewelled eggs, was going to think about it and Suki, the lady who did paper quilling, had politely declined.

Then Flick had spent the rest of the day cleaning the gift shop ready for the delivery in the next day or so. She was knackered.

She had done her best to avoid Luke for the rest of the day. She didn't want to talk about that kiss and how she'd read too much into it. She didn't want to hear him dismiss it and she didn't want to tell him she thought she might be falling in love with him because that was ridiculous. Although she knew he had occupied many of her thoughts that afternoon. And what if he wanted to kiss her again, as part of the charade? How could she do that and keep her heart locked away? And what if he never wanted to kiss her again? That might be infinitely worse.

Urgh, why was she feeling like a silly teenager around him?

Luke was in the kitchen cooking when she walked in and he gave her a small tentative smile as she closed the door behind her. God, it was already awkward. Did he think she was going to throw herself at him again?

'Hey, I made dinner,' Luke gestured to the oven. 'Lasagne, hope that's OK?'

'It smells delicious, thank you.'

He nodded, pushing his hand through his hair as if he wanted to say something but couldn't find the words. Was he going to talk about the kiss? She wasn't ready for that if he was. She'd much rather be an ostrich and stick her head in the sand and pretend it had never happened than talk about it like a grown-up.

She quickly leapt in before he could bring it up. 'I've arranged a workshop for Thursday, a wood-carving one. I hope that's OK? I put a post out asking if anyone affected by a brain injury was interested in doing a workshop and we've had one man sign up already. I thought just working with one person might be a good place to start. I can arrange a phone call with someone from Headway for you, maybe tomorrow or Wednesday, and make sure we're ready for them and you can ask any questions you want. But I wanted to start with you because out of all the artists you were the one most open about teaching the workshops. Is that OK?'

'Yeah of course. I want to be a part of that, at least while I'm here. I'm happy to help in any way I can.'

'Thank you.'

There was silence and she knew he was going to bring it up. She cast around for another topic of conversation. Anything but that, but her mind was blank.

'I, umm... I wanted to talk about the kiss,' Luke said, not meeting her eye.

'Oh there's no need,' Flick said.

She begged him silently not to continue that topic of conversation but he obviously couldn't hear her so he ploughed on regardless.

'I don't want to fake kiss you anymore.'

Oh god, the humiliation and pain.

'Oh of course, that's fine. We probably got the message across with that one kiss. We don't want to overegg the pudding.'

'No Flick, I—'

'Why endure something you didn't enjoy when we've already made the point?'

He stared at her. 'You... didn't enjoy it? You, erm... you said it was the hottest kiss of your life.'

'Yes, well, that was probably a slight overexaggeration.'

'Right.'

'And you clearly didn't enjoy it if once was more than enough.'

'Flick, I think you've misunderstood. I—'

'No misunderstanding. You were very emphatic today that the kiss wasn't real and now you're saying you never want to do it again. I think you've been perfectly clear. And I don't want to kiss you again either. It will just become awkward and weird between us and someone will get hurt. We're probably best just being friends anyway. We work together, we live together, we don't want to blur the lines. It's best we just draw a line under it and pretend it never happened.'

'Right… yes of course.'

She suddenly noticed the bouquet of flowers on the countertop behind him and frowned in confusion. Had he bought her flowers?

'Who are the flowers for?'

He turned to face them, blinking in surprise as if he'd forgotten they were there. 'Oh, erm… my mum. It's her birthday tomorrow so I was going to take some flowers to her grave.'

'That's sweet.'

He nodded. 'So, I have to go out and meet a friend so I'll probably see you tomorrow.'

'What about dinner?'

'I'm not hungry, but please help yourself. There's some garlic bread in the oven too and some salad in the fridge.' He shrugged on his jacket. 'I'm probably going to be out for most of the day tomorrow as well.'

'OK.'

With that he walked out without saying another word. Flick stared after him in confusion. Had she said the wrong thing?

She wandered over to the oven and peered inside. The lasagne, bubbling away nicely, was big enough to feed four people. There were two garlic baguettes slowly turning a golden shade. He'd definitely intended to eat with her.

She cursed herself. She'd clearly pushed it too far saying the kiss wasn't enjoyable and hurt his feelings. But then, he'd hurt her too. *I don't want to kiss you anymore.* Talk about direct and to the point.

She sighed. She said she didn't want to make it weird or awkward between them but she'd definitely already done that.

CHAPTER EIGHT

Flick woke very early the next morning when she heard a thump from the lounge. She looked at the time to see it was six in the morning. She'd stayed up until midnight the night before in the hope of seeing Luke and being able to talk to him but he hadn't come home. She really wanted to clear the air between them and apologise if she'd hurt him.

She scrambled out of bed and quickly went into the lounge and it was evident he was on his way out. His shoulders dropped when he saw her; he clearly didn't want to see her. He looked really sad and then she spotted the flowers in his hand. Of course he'd be sad as today was his mum's birthday.

'Hey,' she said, softly.

'Hi.'

'You're up early.'

'I have lots to do today.'

'Luke, I just want to say…' She watched him glance

down to the flowers and she stopped. Now wasn't the time to talk about that. 'Did you want me to come with you to your mum's grave?'

His eyes widened in horror. 'Why would you want to do that?'

'Because I don't want you to be sad and alone.'

He stared at her. 'You're so lovely,' he said, wistfully. 'And I don't deserve it.'

'What? Of course you do.'

'Thank you for the offer but I'll be OK.'

'Of course. I understand. Grieving is a personal thing, I get that. But if you want to talk or even need a hug when you get back, I'm here for you.'

'Thank you, that's really very kind. I need to go, I'll catch you later.'

He walked out, his head bent as if he was carrying the weight of the world on his shoulders.

∼

Luke walked down the stairs to his car, which he'd loaded with his stag sculpture the night before. He was going to hell. He hated lying and he'd lied to the sweetest, kindest person he'd ever met. It felt like kicking a puppy.

He got in the car and drove down the road. He spotted an elderly lady walking her tiny dog on the side of the road. He pulled over and leaned out the window, offering out the bunch of flowers.

'Here you go, lovely.'

She stared at the flowers in shock. 'What are these for?'

'To make you smile.'

She looked at them suspiciously. 'Did you buy them for a girl and she didn't want them?'

Luke sighed. 'Something like that.'

'The girl's an idiot. You're a nice boy.' She took the flowers from him and a big smile spread across her face.

'Well, I've been told that's the problem,' Luke said, thinking of his ex-girlfriend. She'd thought he was too nice.

'Oh, the old adage of "Treat them mean, keep them keen" doesn't really ring true. That might be exciting to start off with, but no one wants to marry someone like that. You marry your soul mate, someone there for you through the good times and the bad, someone who has your back. Someone who fills your heart to the top. No one wants to fill their hearts with an arsehole.'

'No, I agree.'

'This girl who turned down your flowers, do you love her?'

Luke was regretting choosing this woman for his cast-off flowers. 'I think it's probably a little early for that.'

Although that probably wasn't true. Hearing Flick's offer to accompany him to his mum's grave, or to give him a hug if he needed it, had made him fall for her that little bit more.

The woman looked at him as if she didn't believe that. 'When you know, you know. Did you tell her?'

'I... didn't really get a chance.'

'You tell her you love her and that will mean more to her than a bunch of flowers.'

Luke didn't think he'd ever be brave enough for that. Martine, the last woman he'd said *I love you to*, had laughed and promptly dumped him. In fact, that had happened with the last two women he'd dated, although Sophie had at least been a lot kinder about not loving him before she'd dumped him. 'Thanks for the advice. You have a good day.'

'I will now,' she waved the flowers at him. 'Thank you.'

He smiled and drove off. Maybe if there were some kind of universal points system for being good and bad, making an elderly lady smile with flowers might help counteract the lie he'd told Flick.

∼

Flick was sitting in her empty gift shop busily making her little wish jars later that morning. It was a delicate operation, she didn't want to lose any of the little fluffy seed heads. She was very carefully threading the wire through a dandelion stem to make it stand up when Aidan walked in.

'There's a massive delivery downstairs. Someone needs to come and deal with it.'

That someone clearly was her.

'OK, thanks. I'll be down in two seconds.'

She pushed the wire carefully into the head.

'There are fifty boxes stacked up inside the entrance. It's causing a fire hazard.'

'I don't think there'll be a fire in the next few minutes.'

'You don't know that. A fire can start at any time.'

'From Ethel sewing too fast perhaps? Or the sun coming through the windows and hitting Katherine's glass mosaics in the wrong way?'

'I don't think there is any need to be sarcastic,' Aidan said. 'I'm merely asking you to come and deal with the delivery that is causing an obstruction.'

'And I've said I'll be there in a minute.'

'I guess faffing around with weeds is more important than the health and safety of your staff.'

Flick sighed and stuck the end of the wire in a lump of Blu Tack so it didn't fall over. 'I'll come and deal with it now. I'd never forgive myself if everyone died in a towering inferno.'

Aidan grunted his displeasure at her sarcasm and stomped off back down the stairs, muttering to himself.

Flick had kind of hoped that with the suggestion of running the workshops for those people with brain injuries, the artists would rally behind her. That was what her grandad had been passionate about and he'd instilled a passion about it with the artists too. But there had been a total mixed response. Katherine had been really enthusiastic about it, Rose had agreed to do it although she was worried whether she was capable enough to be trusted with something so important. Ethel and Aidan hadn't wanted to do it at all but had reluctantly agreed with lots of moaning and huffing about it under their breaths. What would it take to make them care?

She went downstairs and glanced into Luke's studio as she approached the front door. It was empty and in darkness. She couldn't help wondering if he was avoiding her.

She got to the front door and Aidan was clearly not exaggerating, there were at least fifty boxes stacked up in the hall. Although all the boxes were addressed to Luke she recognised the names of the suppliers – this must be the stuff she had asked Luke to order for her. She started taking the boxes upstairs. While most of them were quite light, a few were heavy and the gift shop was two floors up. It would be nice if some of the other artists helped her but she didn't feel she had the kind of relationship with them that would allow her to ask them.

After getting the final box upstairs, she started to unpack and felt like a kid on Christmas morning opening all the boxes and finding homes for the products around the empty gift shop. She decided to have all the craft paraphernalia and kits on the bottom floor of the gift shop as that was what she was most passionate about. All the rest of the gifts were going to be upstairs on the mezzanine. A lot of the shelving and tables for the middle of the shop hadn't arrived yet so she couldn't find homes for everything but it was a great start.

She felt so happy that she was finally doing this. Opening a craft supplies shop had always been her dream and, thanks to Luke persuading her to do it, it was finally coming true. She was going to give it her all. If it all came crashing down in six months, no one could say she hadn't given it her best shot.

Although she still felt like she needed to clear the air with him after the night before. She took a few pictures of her beautifully presented shelves and sent them to Luke with the message: 'I'm so happy right now, thank you for pushing me to do this.'

He texted straight back. 'I'm glad I can make you happy.' Then he sent another text. 'Sorry I wasn't there to help you with the boxes.'

She smiled. That was Luke all over. She really hoped he would be back soon and she could make things right between them.

~

Luke climbed up the steps to the roof and sighed when he realised it was already occupied. He'd been successfully avoiding Flick all day, although he knew he couldn't do that long term. He'd have to face her at some point.

'Hey, I haven't seen you all day. Are you OK?' Flick asked and he hated the uncertainty in her eyes.

'Yeah, I had to deliver the stag now that it's finished and then I went shopping for some of the things that Polly needs for the café.'

'Oh, I thought you were avoiding me,' Flick laughed.

'I even checked the cupboard a few times to see if you were hiding from me in there.'

He didn't know how to answer that because although what he'd said about where he'd been was true he had deliberately done those things so he wouldn't have to be around the studios and see her.

He sat down next to her. She looked out over the town and was quiet for a moment.

'Big storm coming tonight,' she said, clearly desperately trying to fill the awkward silence. 'Eighty-mile-an-hour winds apparently. You wouldn't think that was likely judging by how calm it is out there right now.'

He cleared his throat. 'Yes, it's going to be bad. I hope our wonky tree will be OK.'

'Oh, that tree will be there forever.'

They lapsed into awkward silence again and he hated this. He wished he could take that kiss back although he knew in his heart he couldn't regret the best damn kiss of his life.

'How has today been?' she asked gently. 'I've been thinking about you. Did you go to your mum's grave?'

He hated lying. The lie about the flowers had slipped off the tongue so easily the night before to save his embarrassment but he wasn't going to dine out on the lie just to get himself some sympathy.

To his surprise, she slipped her hand into his. 'If you want to talk about it, I'm here for you.'

Enough was enough.

'Flick, I lied about the flowers.'

Her face fell and she quickly removed her hand. 'What?'

'It's not her birthday today, not even close. And she doesn't even have a grave, she was cremated and her ashes scattered in the sea, so even if I wanted to take her flowers, I'd have nowhere to do that.'

Hurt filled her eyes. 'Why would you lie over something like that?'

'I didn't do it for sympathy if that's what you're thinking. You asked me about the flowers and I had to come up with a lie and that was the first thing I thought of. If I'd had more time I'd have said they were for a sick friend or something. I didn't realise you were going to be all sweet and lovely and sympathetic about it. I'm sorry.'

'I don't understand. Why would you need to lie about the flowers in the first place?'

'Because I bought them for you.'

Her eyes widened in shock and he couldn't face any more questions so he got up and went back downstairs. But she was hot on his heels and she caught up with him just as he was heading towards his bedroom.

'Luke, why did you buy me flowers?'

He sighed. The can of worms was well and truly open now. He might as well give the can a good shake and empty out all the worms for her to see.

'Because I like you, a lot more than I should. And not just because of the earth-shattering kiss, but because you're lovely and kind and like sunshine on a rainy day.

And because you like me for who I am not... other reasons.'

She stared at him in confusion. 'But last night you said you didn't want to kiss me anymore.'

'I said I didn't want to *fake* kiss you anymore. I was going to ask you out on a real date. Hence the dinner and the flowers.'

She stared at him in horror. Well there was his answer.

'You... you were going to ask me out? For real?'

'Yes.'

'But... you're moving. To the Isle of Skye. That's nearly fourteen hours away. I checked.'

He frowned. Why had she checked?

'I know, but I felt like we had some kind of connection, even before the kiss, and I knew if I walked away from here in a few weeks and never explored this spark between us, I would always regret it.'

She watched him like he was a complicated maths problem she was trying to solve.

'Look, it doesn't matter. It's just a silly crush, it doesn't have to be weird between us,' Luke said.

'Oh, we're already there.'

He sighed. 'I know. But it will all be fine in a few days. I'll get over it and we can just get back to being friends again. Goodnight Flick.'

He turned for his bedroom but she snagged his arm. 'We're not done here.' She stepped closer. 'Yesterday, after our... incredible kiss...'

His heart leapt. Had it really been incredible for her too?

'You were all, oh but it's not real, it doesn't mean anything,' Flick said.

'You said it didn't mean anything. I never said that.'

'Because you said it wasn't real.'

He sighed because they were going round in circles here.

'And I was gutted because… it was the best kiss of my entire life and you were just dismissing it,' Flick said.

His heart soared, his mouth suddenly dry. 'Flick, are you saying… Do you like me too?'

She smiled. 'Way too much.'

He laughed with relief. 'God, there's a lot to be said for simple honest conversations.'

She reached up to stroke his face. 'And not jumping to conclusions. I should have let you speak last night but I was so hurt and embarrassed when you said you didn't want to kiss me anymore.'

'I probably could have opened with something more positive.' He leaned his forehead against hers.

'And for the record, I didn't need flowers or for you to cook me dinner for me to say yes. All I needed was for you to kiss me again like you did yesterday and I'd have been yours.'

He smiled with relief and cupped her face. 'Is it too late?'

She wrapped her arms around him. 'Definitely not.'

He bent his head to kiss her then pulled back. 'And I

know I'm leaving in a few weeks and I don't know what will happen then but—'

'We worry about tomorrow, tomorrow. We have no idea where this will go, that spark between us might well and truly have fizzled out by the time you leave, but we can have a lot of fun together over the next few weeks while we get to know each other better.'

That sounded a bit more casual than he would like but she was right. A lot could happen in a few weeks. She might decide he was too nice and boring for one, his previous girlfriends had. He just had to enjoy what was happening now and not worry about anything else.

With his heart thundering against his chest, he bent his head and kissed her.

CHAPTER NINE

Luke's kiss was slow at first, gentle and respectful which made her smile against his lips because that was Luke all over. He was just so bloody lovely.

Flick wanted to laugh and cry in relief. He liked her and they could have so easily missed this opportunity because they were both afraid of getting hurt.

She moved her hands round the back of his neck, pressing herself up tighter against him and relishing in the feel of his solid, warm body against hers. She stroked her fingers through his hair and he made a rumbly noise of appreciation at the back of his throat that ignited something deep inside of her.

As if reading her mind, he pulled back fractionally. 'Shall we take this in there?' he gestured to his bedroom. 'We might be a little more comfortable.'

There was a significant height difference between the two of them so she knew he was only being practical, but the thought of him pinning her to his bed while he kissed her filled her with joy. Hell, the thought of him making love to her in his bed made her bubble with so much excitement and it had been a long time since she'd felt that way about anyone. Nerves suddenly flooded her. It *had* been a long time since she'd done that.

He took her delay in answering as hesitation. 'We don't have to do anything but kiss. Or we can stay out here if that makes you more comfortable.'

And with those words every nerve vanished. This was Luke, he would be nothing but kind.

She leaned up and kissed him again. 'Take me to bed.'

He smiled against her lips as he kissed her and then bent down and scooped her up, much to her delight, and carried her to his bed. He laid her down and then lay down next to her, taking her face in his hand and kissing her again with slow, gentle, loving kisses. She moved her mouth to his neck, trailing kisses down his throat and she felt the moan vibrating against her lips. When he kissed her again, it was suddenly a lot more passionate and needful and he rolled slightly on top of her. She could instantly feel how turned on he was and the thought that she'd had that effect on him simply from a kiss was such a thrill. But despite how much he clearly wanted her, he didn't take it any further than a kiss. His hands never wandered, his mouth stayed on hers. He was happy just kissing and, while she loved him a little bit for that, her body was humming with need.

She slid her hands underneath his t-shirt, stroking his back, enjoying the feel of his muscles in his shoulders and how the kiss changed too because of her touch. She moved her hands to the hem and pulled the t-shirt over his head, and he paused kissing her so she could remove it.

She stroked his face and he stared down at her with such affection. 'Would you like me to undress you?'

She nodded keenly.

He reached down to the hem of her dress and slowly slid it up her thighs, his hand caressing her bare leg as he did so. She let out a moan at how close he was to where she needed him and yet still too far away. He pushed her dress up over her stomach and he kissed there as the skin was exposed. It was so sweet and so very hot. He pulled the dress over her head and his eyes feasted on her body. It made her feel so adored.

He slowly peeled down her knickers and she helped him by lifting her bum and then quickly removed her bra. He stared at her for a moment, taking her in before he kissed her hard. The feel of his skin against hers was wonderful but she cried out in relief when he slid a hand up the inside of her thigh and touched her in the exact place she needed him.

He pulled back to look at her, his eyes filled with concern at the noise she made.

'Is this OK?'

'Yes, god yes, don't stop.'

He smiled and moved his hand slightly. 'What about this?'

She let out a noise that was pure gibberish as she gripped his shoulder and he laughed. 'I'll take that as a yes.'

'It's definitely a yes.'

He kissed her again, touching her and stroking her, somehow knowing her body better than she did. He took her higher and higher until she soared over the edge, shouting out against his lips and clinging to him like he was a life raft and she'd been lost at sea.

He pulled back and kissed her on the forehead, so sweetly. And then moved his mouth to her neck. She stroked the back of his neck as she came down from her high, trying to catch her breath. She felt relaxed now, he'd taken away that frantic need. He could kiss her for the rest of the night without her climbing the walls desperate for that release.

He moved his mouth to her shoulder and then across her chest, taking her breast between his lips and she cried out again, that feeling instantly starting to build again.

'Luke, oh my god.'

She felt him smile against her breast before he moved his mouth lower across her belly and then between her legs. She stared at him in shock. She hadn't slept with that many men, and the last one had put her off sex for the last few years, but foreplay had never rated very highly for any of them. But for Luke, he was clearly enjoying what he could do for her rather than what she could do for him.

And then all thoughts went out the window as he did wonderful things with his tongue. That feeling coiled quickly in her stomach and built so fast and hard, her orgasm slamming into her as she arched her back and clawed at the sheets.

He moved back over her and her breath was ragged as he kissed her. He pulled back and stroked her hair from her face. 'We don't have to go any further than this. You don't owe me anything. I'll be very happy just kissing you for the rest of the night if you don't want to go any further.'

She smiled and shook her head. 'I want you. All of you.'

He nodded and she helped him out of his jeans and shorts so they were both naked.

She stroked his face and kissed him.

She pulled back to look at him. 'Where have you been, Luke Donnelly?'

'I've been right here, waiting for you.'

She smiled at that. 'Make love to me.'

He nodded and reached over to the drawers to grab a condom. She took it off him, ripped it open and slowly rolled it on, loving the feel of him in her hand and the effect her touching him clearly had on him.

He leaned over her, gathering her legs around his hips, and moved very carefully inside her. She wrapped her arms around his neck, relishing in the feel of his chest against hers. She stared up into his eyes as he started moving slowly against her. Sex for her had always been fast and over very quickly but he was taking his time, clearly enjoying every stroke, every touch. He was in no rush and she loved that.

She ran her hands down his back, her fingers tracing the indent of his spine.

'Is this OK?' Luke asked.

She let out a sigh of blissful contentment. 'It's lovely.'

He paused and a frown crossed his face. 'We could change positions or I could—'

She caught his face in her hands. 'Luke, I don't want to change a thing, this is utter perfection.'

'Well,' he let out a huff of relief. 'Perfection sounds a lot better than lovely.'

She laughed. 'You are the most incredible man I've ever met and I honestly couldn't be happier right now.'

He carried on moving against her and it was utterly divine.

'And you don't need to wait for me, you've already given me two toe-curling orgasms, it's your turn.'

He smiled. 'It doesn't work like that. Besides, I'm just getting started.'

She let her fingers play against his back. She wasn't sure she had another orgasm in her but then he seemed to change his angle slightly which made her gasp with surprise. He kissed her, shifting her legs higher round his waist, and the feel of him made her moan against his lips. He moved his mouth to her neck, the sensitive spot right below her ear, and she clung to his shoulders, that feeling building in her already, spreading out to every part of her body as if little fireworks were going off everywhere. He moved his mouth to her breast and she arched against him as that feeling tightened in her stomach. Then he moved his mouth to her heart, giving her a long, lingering kiss right there and it was so sweet, so loving, it completely unravelled her. When he pulled back to look at her, it was the look of adoration and maybe even love that sent her spiralling over the edge, taking him with her. She shouted out his name before he kissed her hard, holding her tight as she fell apart.

∽

The storm was raging outside, wind roaring through the roof tiles making them rattle. Rain was thundering so hard against the roof and windows, Flick wouldn't be surprised if she woke up tomorrow and found the house had been taken to Oz but right then she couldn't be happier as she lay cuddled up next to Luke.

'I can't believe we're here,' Luke said.

Flick snorted with laughter. 'Mutually agreed nakedness.'

He laughed. 'Oh, yes, I think my inappropriate crush had started even then. I never say the right things when I like a woman, I become a bumbling mess.'

'I like your bumbling mess. Everything about you is just so damned likeable, I like you exactly how you are and I've liked you for a while too. I thought you were going to kiss me in the secret cupboard and I really wanted that but then you backed away. Why?'

'Because I'd bundled you in a cupboard and told you to be quiet. Kissing you under those circumstances didn't feel very… consensual.'

She smiled as her heart filled with love for him. He really was the loveliest man she'd ever met.

'And I never imagined you would like me back,' Luke said. 'That seemed too good to be true.'

'Why would you doubt that? You're lovely, kind, funny. Amazing in bed.'

He laughed and then frowned. 'I haven't had the greatest track record when it comes to women. I've had two semi-serious relationships. I loved them both but they didn't return those feelings.'

'Oh Luke.'

'It's OK, it's just the way things work out sometimes. But I suppose it dented my confidence. With Sophie, we were friends long before we started sleeping together. And we had so much fun hanging out. Looking back I don't think it was much more than friends with benefits but I loved her so much. After a few months I told her I loved her and she smiled and stroked me on the cheek and said she would never see me as anything more than a friend. I was heartbroken. And then there was Martine. Now that was a toxic relationship. She was a one-night stand that dragged on for months. I was smitten. I cringe now when I think about her. I have no idea what I saw in her but she really didn't like or respect me and I don't know why I stayed as long as I did when she belittled everything I did. She kept telling me that I could never get anyone better than her, that no one else would ever want me, and I guess I just started to believe it. She dumped me when I told her I loved her. She laughed and said I was too nice and boring for her.'

'I'm so sorry, what a horrible thing to say to someone. And you're not boring, not at all. I love being around you and talking to you or watching you work. But this sounds like her issue not yours. She would probably be much better suited to someone like my ex, Ryan, than I was. He was pretty toxic too. He liked weird stuff in the bedroom, she probably would have liked that. But dumping you meant she missed out on being with the most incredible man I've ever met.'

Luke smiled and kissed her. 'Thank you.'

'So I'm guessing sex wasn't particularly fun with her either.'

'No, she was always criticising or laughing at what I was doing.'

'Christ, I imagine that left your confidence in tatters.'

'I haven't been with a woman since Martine. I didn't feel like I had anything to offer.'

'Is that why you've been avoiding Natalia and the other women?'

'No, that's… I don't think they particularly like me either.'

Flick frowned in confusion. 'Luke, you have nothing to worry about in the bedroom department. What we shared was… magnificent.'

A smile lit up his face. 'Really?'

She nodded. 'You've definitely helped me back on the horse. I haven't been with another man since Ryan. I've dated other men, but I haven't slept with anyone.'

'Tell me about him. What happened with him that put you off being with another man?'

'So many things. Like you, I don't know what I saw in him. He was really sweet to start with, he was so attentive and charming, always saying nice things. He'd take me out for dinner or nice days out. He was always ringing me, texting me, wanting to spend time with me. It was so different to how my previous boyfriend, Charlie, had been where I barely saw him and he almost never messaged me. I guess I was flattered by the attention, but even at the beginning I thought it was a bit too much, sometimes I'd get fifty messages a day from him.'

She absently stroked a finger across his chest. 'Although there were other red flags, I chose to ignore. He wanted me to cancel plans with friends to spend time with him which I didn't and he wasn't happy about that. He'd get so sulky if I didn't do the things he wanted me to do. He was used to getting his own way. He grew up rich and if he wanted a pony or a quad bike or the latest game console, his mum would get it. He was spoiled and entitled about everything in his life, including me. He was so ridiculously rich. Although I didn't know that when we started dating. If I'd known, I'd probably have avoided him like the plague.'

'You don't like rich people? What if I was to tell you that I'm secretly rich and famous?'

She smiled at the joke. 'Thank god you're not. Living in London there's a lot of rich pretentious people there and most of them are complete arseholes. From experience they have such a huge sense of entitlement. They feel like things should be handed to them on a platter just because Daddy's rich. Ryan would buy me things, stupid expensive things, and then expect me to have sex with him and get very irate when I didn't want to.'

'Flick, that's horrible.'

'I know, I just wasn't comfortable enough with him to want to sleep with him. That should have been a red flag in itself. I guess my subconscious was trying to tell me not to trust him so I kept telling him I wanted more time. The more he pestered me about it, the more I pulled away. I think he saw it as a bit of a challenge and bought me more things: a diamond necklace, ruby earrings, it was ridiculous, I didn't want any of them. I never wore stuff like that, not just because I couldn't afford it but it wasn't my style. I'd wear a starfish necklace or one with a dragon or a seahorse. I don't even have my ears pierced so earrings were a bit useless.'

She shook her head as she remembered. 'I know I sound so ungrateful but the things he bought me weren't for me anyway, they were for him. I've always dressed in bright colours but he said black was classier so he'd buy me black designer dresses, black shoes, black handbags and get very upset when I didn't want to wear them. It was the oddest relationship. I kept on thinking why is he with me if he doesn't like me the way I am. But he could turn on the charm when he wanted to. Every time he could see that I was pulling away, he'd pull out the charm and compliments, tell me how beautiful I was, how much he loved me, how he was one of the richest people in the UK and could have any woman in the world and he'd chosen me. It made me feel incredibly flattered. He said he only wanted to make me happy and didn't I want to make him happy too. He said wearing a black dress was such a small thing and he made me feel silly for protesting against it. So I wore the clothes he bought me when we went on dates but looking back I started losing who I was. And then there was the sofa and I'm still angry about that.'

'What happened to the sofa?'

'I had this beautiful peacock-blue sofa with these gorgeous cushions that had peacock feathers in golds and greens. It was second hand when I bought it so it was a little threadbare on the arms but I had all these blue and green accessories in the flat to go with it. And it was so soft and luxurious to sit on. I loved it. Every time I'd walk through the door of my flat it made me smile. One day I came home to find he had replaced it with a very dull, dark grey one. I was horrified. He took my spare key from my overly trusting neighbour and just got rid of my beloved sofa. He never even asked me. I was so angry. He knew how much I loved that sofa because he mocked it when he first saw it and said it belonged in a brothel. I told him it was the most beautiful sofa in the world and it was my most favourite thing I owned. And he just threw it away. We had this big row where he said I was so ungrateful and behaving like a child and after he stormed out, I was left feeling like I was being unreasonable. He had perfected the art of gaslighting and I ended up ringing *him* and apologising. He said that everything he did for me wasn't good enough and he didn't think I loved him because I never wanted to be intimate with him.

He basically guilted me into agreeing to sleep with him.'

'This guy is giving me the creeps and I haven't even met him.'

'I know. Tabitha calls him Red Flag Ryan and he really was. So we meet up the next night, have dinner at a hundred miles an hour because he's rushing me. He takes me back to his place and as soon as we step through the door he was all over me. It was like a lion mauling his prey. He literally tore off the dress I was wearing. Thankfully, it was one of the horrible black ones he'd bought me not one of mine. So I'm naked on the bed, he's still fully clothed, he's kissing me and grabbing me like he's never seen a naked woman before and he doesn't know what to do, I'm trying to slow him down and suddenly he leans over and pulls out a pair of handcuffs.'

'What? I mean I know some people like that kind of thing, but surely there should have been some kind of conversation about it before he springs them on you.'

'Exactly. I had no idea he was into that sort of thing. I thought he was going to grab a condom. He said he wants to have sex with me handcuffed me to the headboard. I absolutely did not want to do that. It wasn't something I'd done before or even wanted to. He got so sulky and annoyed when I said no. He said I was immature and that women loved been tied up or handcuffed. He made me feel like there was something wrong with me for saying no. He said if I trusted him I'd let him do it. The thing was I didn't trust him, I just couldn't tell him that. Looking back I don't know why I let him badger me into doing it, why I wasn't strong enough to stand by my answer. But he was pleading with me and telling me I'd really enjoy it and so I caved and I hate that I did. He handcuffed me to the headboard and the second they were on he gave me such a triumphant look. He said he was in control now and he could do anything he wanted with me.'

She realised Luke was stroking her back and she looked up at this kind, wonderful, brilliant man and couldn't help but smile. She felt so incredibly lucky to be lying here next to him. Whenever she'd spoken about this before, she'd always felt that panic rise up in her as she relived that night but she didn't feel that way now. She had never felt so completely safe as she did right now cuddled up in his arms.

'He starts to undress and he's staring at me the whole time with this cold look in his eyes, there was no affection there, it really started to freak me out. He comes back to the bed and pulls out a blindfold. I said there was no way I was wearing that and he laughed and put it on me anyway. It was horrible. I hated feeling so vulnerable, I could barely move, I couldn't see, my heart was beating so fast that I thought I was going to pass out. I told him to stop, that I didn't want this.'

'Did he stop?'

'Not right away.'

'What the hell does that mean?'

'Well he carried on touching me for about another five seconds and by this time full-blown panic kicks in that he isn't going to stop at all and I start screaming at him. He stopped pretty quick after that and he undid the handcuffs. But he said I obviously didn't trust him and I told him I didn't and that was it, after several cross words, we were over. The next day I parcelled up every single gift he'd given me, the ridiculously expensive jewellery, the clothes and sent them all back. I contacted a local charity to remove the sofa and tried not to think about him ever again. I felt nothing but relief that it was over.'

'I'm so sorry you went through that. I can understand why it scared you.'

'Oh, he probably wouldn't have done anything bad. He phoned me the next day to apologise, he said he thought that being an alpha male was what women wanted. I told him being an alpha didn't mean he had to be a dick.'

'Yes exactly. Sex should always be fully consensual, especially when dabbling with stuff like that. He should never have badgered you into it when he could see you weren't happy about it. And stop means stop, no matter what.'

She smiled and stroked his face. 'It would have been very different if I'd done that kind of thing with you.'

'Yes, if I'd brought out handcuffs during sex and you looked even remotely turned off by the idea, the handcuffs would be going in the bin. But I have no desire to control you or be in charge in or outside the bedroom, so we'd probably never be having that conversation about handcuffs anyway. Besides, I liked you touching me when we made love, so I'm not sure what kind of pleasure I'd get from handcuffing you, I'd be missing out more than anything.'

She smiled at that.

'So Ryan was the last person you slept with?'

'Well technically no, we never got that far. But I've dated a few men since then and I've always ended it before it got anywhere because the thought of sex made me think of him and that night and I start to panic all over again.'

'Why was it different with me?'

'Because I trusted you completely. Because you have been nothing but kind since we first met. You think nice and lovely aren't compliments because your ex-girlfriend made you think they were something bad or something to be ashamed of. But they aren't. You are wonderful and I couldn't have done it with you if you weren't.'

'I wish you'd told me you were nervous about sex before we did it. I would have been more careful.'

Her eyebrows shot up at that. 'There is nothing you could have done to make it better for me. You were kind, respectful, gentle, and quite honestly it was the best sex I've ever had, because of that.'

He smiled and kissed her. 'For me too.'

She smiled at that.

He stroked her face. 'So I can understand why you were put off sex after what Ryan did but it doesn't really explain your hatred for rich people. Ryan didn't act that way because he was rich, he acted that way because he was a dick. I'm not sure you can tar all rich people with the same brush. I'm sure some of them are nice.'

'I suppose, although I'm yet to meet a nice one and I certainly would be wary about being involved with someone so rich again.'

Luke was silent for a moment. 'Well, I think you should try to keep an open mind.'

She wasn't sure why he was focussing on that but she could see this was important to him. 'OK, I'll try.'

He looked worried and she didn't know why. 'Are you OK?'

'Yes, I'm fine, couldn't be happier.'

She didn't think he was being entirely truthful about that but as she was about to ask him about it he kissed her. 'I'm so damned happy,' he whispered against her lips before kissing her again, so sweetly, so passionately that she forgot everything else.

CHAPTER TEN

Flick was busily helping Luke put together the newly delivered shelves the next day. Well, helping was probably a bit generous as he was doing most of the work. If she were putting them together they would be wonky, loose and fall apart after a few hours. But she was passing him screws and giving him moral support so she was helping a little.

'I need a few more tools, I'll be back in a sec,' Luke said, getting up from where he was kneeling on the floor. He walked past her then doubled back and gave her the sweetest kiss before disappearing out of the gift shop door.

Flick stood up and wandered over to the archway to check on Polly. All the gadgets and machines had been delivered and Polly's boyfriend was now busily installing all of them for her. The room had been painted in yellow and Rose was working away at the back of the room adding bees, flowers and grass to the walls. The new tables and chairs had been delivered and looked fantastic. The new countertop hadn't arrived yet but apart from that Polly looked almost ready to go.

Polly saw her standing there and waved her over.

'How's it going?' Flick asked.

'Good, really good,' Polly said, excitedly. 'Honestly, this is a dream come true for me, I can't tell you how happy I am and I want to thank you, and Luke obviously, for making my dreams a reality.'

'You don't need to thank me,' Flick said. 'Just seeing this place be a success will be thanks enough. If this works, there'll be more people coming through the door and that can only be a good thing for the studios and artists.'

'I hope so. It feels like a lot of pressure to get it right. If I fail, the whole studio fails.'

'It won't be your fault if the studios close. The artists are so set in their ways that this place has been dying for years. It will be them who will be the making or breaking of the studios and their willingness to get behind the change.'

Polly nodded. 'I thought I might do a bit of a soft launch tomorrow, just coffee, teas and cake. I thought I'd put a post out on Facebook asking people to come and test the cakes. Buy a drink and get a free slice of cake in return for honest feedback. It will just get people through the door and let them know what we're doing up here so everyone knows that change is coming. I know the new countertops aren't here yet but Rose is practically finished and I'm going to make sure the place is spotless this afternoon.'

'That sounds like a great idea. The more buzz we can create around this place the better. I think the grand opening is likely to be next week but there's no reason why we can't start getting people through the doors now.'

Polly nodded. 'Also I love what you are doing with the art therapy workshops for those with brain injuries. Although I have nothing to contribute in terms of teaching art, I will donate free drinks, cake and sandwiches for every workshop.'

'Wow, Polly, thank you, that's really generous.'

'I think it's something important to be a part of.'

'I do too. Our first one is tomorrow. Just one man and his husband. I'm crossing everything it goes well.'

Just then Flick's phone rang. 'Sorry, I should get this.'

Flick looked at the phone as she moved back into the gift shop. It was a foreign number but she was pretty sure the country code was Australian so she answered it anyway.

'Flick!' came her nan's cheerful voice from the other end of the phone. 'How are you?'

'I'm good,' Flick said with a smile as she thought about Luke. 'How's Aunty Edith?' Technically Edith was her great-aunt but she never called her that.

'She's doing well, starting to hobble around a bit. It's a long road. And if you speak to her, you can't tell her what I'm about to tell you.'

'My lips are sealed.'

'She has the hottest young carer who comes every day to help her. Well I say young, he's probably in his fifties but that's still a lot younger than me and he is so fit and strong. I've never looked at anyone since your grandad passed, but Maxwell has certainly opened my eyes. I don't want to go into specifics because a lady never kisses and tells but we've had the most incredible sex.'

Flick's eyebrows shot up in surprise but she couldn't help smiling. Her nan sounded so happy and excited. Flick knew how that felt. 'Look at you with your toy boy.'

'Stop it,' Audrey chuckled. 'It's just sex. It doesn't mean anything. He's not going to want something serious with an old bird like me. But I have caught him giving me the eye now and again, looking at me as if he wants more. Unless that's just cataracts.'

Flick laughed. 'And Edith doesn't know?'

'Her house is pretty big and she can't access most of it right now. Let's say there are lots of rooms we can sneak off to when he's finished tending to her. And she sleeps a lot, or she's busy watching her soaps or doing her crosswords. What she doesn't know won't hurt her.'

Flick smiled and shook her head.

'Now tell me, how are you getting on with young Luke?'

'Good, very good,' Flick answered vaguely.

There was a pause on the other end. 'Oh my god you've slept with him.'

'Nan!'

'You have, haven't you?'

'My sex life is private.'

'Dear god, that's wonderful news,' Audrey went on as if Flick had confirmed it, which she probably had. 'He's a lovely boy and he needed someone wonderful. I'm so glad you two have found each other. But I didn't see that coming, let me tell you. Is he good in bed?'

Flick let out a sigh. There was no point denying it anymore. 'Yeah, he is.'

Her nan squealed on the other end of the phone. 'This makes me so happy. For both of you. I'm going to need all the sexy details.'

'I'm afraid you'll have to use your imagination for that one.'

'Spoilsport. OK, I haven't got long, I don't want to run up Edith's phone bill. How is everything going in the studios?'

Flick wanted to tell her how frustrating it was that she'd been left to deliver the bad news to the artists and if her nan had paved the way they might be a little bit more supportive but she decided to focus on the positive instead.

'It's going really well. We're going to reopen the café to start with.'

'Oh no, Flick, I really don't want to have to deal with that when I get home.'

'You won't have to. We found a woman, Polly, who runs a catering service from her van selling burgers, sandwiches, chips and drinks. She's going to take it over and she'll be in charge of everything, ordering food, cooking, serving, hiring staff if needs be. You won't have to lift a finger but we need the café to help get a regular revenue into the place. We're busily renovating it now, painting, new tables and chairs, new utensils and equipment. And I'm going to use the space next door to open a gift shop. I'm going to sell normal gift shop gifts but also I'm going to sell arts and craft supplies so people can have a go at creating their own masterpieces.'

There was silence from her nan which Flick was nervous about. She'd thought she'd be pleased.

'This all sounds lovely, but how are you paying for all this?'

'From the kitty.'

'What kitty?'

'Luke said there was a small kitty to help with anything that needed repairing or any decorating or refurbishments. It was donated by an anonymous donor.'

'Well, that's the first I've bloody heard of it.'

'What?'

'I'm so annoyed,' her nan went on. 'I've always told Luke I didn't want his money.'

'Luke is the anonymous donor?'

'Of course he is. I don't know anyone else who would have thousands of pounds to spend on a new café and other expensive renovations.'

How could Flick have been so stupid? She had suspected he had something to do with it at the beginning but then he'd thrown her off the scent with this anonymous donor business. And she'd believed him.

'Everyone sees him as a cash cow because he's a millionaire but I've always been very clear that I didn't want anything from him,' her nan went on.

'He's... a millionaire?' Flick asked, her voice breaking.

'You didn't know?'

'No.'

'Oh, I thought with you two sleeping together he would have told you. I'm such a romantic. There's me seeing the next big love story and you two are just having sex. Well, why not? You two are young, you deserve some fun. It doesn't always have to be marriage and babies just because you sleep together.'

Flick felt her cheeks heat because her romantic heart had started hoping for that. Not marriage and babies, it was way too soon to think about that, but a big love story. She was falling for Luke so hard and fast. Was this really just sex for him? Why wouldn't he tell her? Did he not trust her?

'Is he really a millionaire or are you exaggerating because he has a few thousand in his bank?'

'He's a millionaire. I have no idea how much he has in the bank. He gives hundreds of thousands away to charities but he's still earning a mint.'

'How?'

'Oh, remember that song that came out about four or five years ago? "Crazy Monkey"?'

'That really annoying song from the phone commercial that ended up being number one in the download chart and the official top forty for most of the year?'

'Yes, Luke wrote it. Or created it. It was all done on the computer. He made it for the phone company but he retained the rights. All royalties from the downloads went to him.'

Flick had no words at all. That song, by a group called Purple Dragon, had been everywhere thanks to the annoyingly catchy tune and the stupid video that accompanied it. There was even a 'Crazy Monkey' dance which everyone knew and would recreate in the clubs and pubs. She'd danced to it herself when going out with her friends in London. There were videos of people doing the dance from all over the world. And there was merchandise, hats, t-shirts, mugs with the silly monkey on it, it was a phenomenon. And while the furore had well and truly died down now, Luke must still be making fairly decent money from it. He'd get money from people watching the video on YouTube, let alone any other revenue streams for it.

Suddenly the penny dropped. That was why Natalia and some of the other women of the town were always sniffing around him. They wanted him for his money. That was why Polly had come out with a massive list of utensils and machines that she absolutely must have because she knew Luke was footing the bill.

Flick felt sick. The list of all the things she had got Luke to buy for the gift shop cost thousands too. She had unknowingly been as bad as everyone else. It would all have to go back, every single thing, and she felt her heart break a little because of that.

She heard a noise behind her and turned round to

see Luke, who judging by his face had heard a good portion of the conversation or at least her side.

'I, umm… I need to go,' Flick said.

'Oh OK. Tell Luke I'm not happy about any of this.'

'I will,' Flick said, weakly. She said her goodbyes and hung up.

'I was going to tell you,' Luke said.

'But you didn't.'

He pushed his hand through his hair. 'I tried to last night.'

She frowned in confusion. 'When did you try?'

'When I said I was secretly rich and famous.'

She scoffed. 'That's not… That's like when people say they are secretly Batman or secretly a witch. No one takes that seriously. That's not how you tell someone you're a millionaire.'

'How do you tell someone?'

She shook her head. 'I don't know, but not like that.'

'It's not easy, believe me.'

'Well when it was obvious I didn't believe you, why didn't you tell me you were telling the truth? Make me believe you.'

'What, when you were going on about how much you hate rich people? Yeah, that felt like the perfect time.'

She realised why he'd been so adamant about some rich people being nice. She had to concede she had probably made it difficult for him to come out with the truth.

'Why didn't you tell me before?'

'I didn't know you before.'

'You knew me well enough to sleep with me.'

'That's different.'

'I'm sure it is, especially when it's just sex. It doesn't matter if you know the person or not.'

'It wasn't just sex.'

'Wasn't it? I trusted you completely to feel comfortable enough to sleep with you, but you didn't trust me at all.'

'I did. I do.'

'So why didn't you tell me before instead of making up the lies about the kitty?'

'I didn't lie as such. I didn't lie when I said there was an anonymous donor. I just didn't tell you the anonymous donor was me.'

'So why didn't you tell me?'

'Because you wouldn't have accepted the money and I wanted to help. I've been very lucky in my life, and I'm living my dream being able to do wood sculptures every day. I wanted to be able to do the same for you. And when would have been a good time to admit the truth? When you walked in on me naked? When I properly introduced myself a few hours later, "Hello, I'm Luke Donnelly and I'm a millionaire"? Everything has moved so quick for us. There just wasn't a right time.'

'You should have found the time.'

He sighed. 'I should have and I'm sorry. But every single person in Lovegrove Bay knows who I am and how much money I have. It's impossible to have any kind of friendship or relationship without wondering whether they like me for me or because of the size of my wallet – and ninety-nine percent of the time it's the latter. That's why I'm leaving because it's just become unbearable. I wanted you to get to know me without any preconceptions.'

'You were testing me?'

'No, not at all.'

'Yes, you were. You wanted to see how I'd act around you when I didn't know you had any money. Well I guess I failed that test, I gave you a list the length of my arm of things I wanted to get for the gift shop. I'm just as bad as Polly and everyone else using you for your money.'

'You didn't know I was footing the bill and you offered to pay me back. No one has ever done that before.'

'Well, everything is going to be sent back. I'll package it all up and send it back today, including these stupid shelves.'

Luke pushed his hand through his hair. 'Now you're being ridiculous.'

'No, I don't want your money. I told you before, throwing money at this isn't the answer.'

'I'm not just throwing money at it. Having the café and the gift shop will get people through the door, which will help the artists to sell their products. It will bring in much needed revenue to support the studios and most importantly will help to fund the workshops for those with brain injuries. This is an investment and one I'm happy to make.'

'Why?'

He frowned. 'You know this place is important to me because it helped my mum after her stroke. I want to save it for her and for your grandad who created such a brilliant legacy of helping other people. And I want to help you, you're passionate about saving it and I can help, so why the hell not?'

Flick folded her arms across her chest, not liking the idea of being beholden to him.

'Your bias against rich people is clouding your view of this. I want to help, there is no ulterior motive here. If you're thinking that I bought you all this because I wanted you to repay me with sex then you don't know me at all. And if you do think that then we need to end this now because I can't be with someone who thinks that little of me. Is that what you think?'

She frowned. Was that what this was? Was her bad experience with Ryan tainting this? Was her subconscious waiting for Luke to demand something in return? No, she knew Luke wasn't like that. She trusted him. She was just annoyed that she'd spent thousands of pounds of his money without realising and it still stung that he hadn't told her.

'I'll take that as a yes,' Luke said and walked out.

'Luke, wait.'

But he didn't and she was left alone feeling frustrated and annoyed.

Flick went looking for Luke later. She was still frustrated that he hadn't told her before and that she'd inadvertently spent thousands of pounds of his money but she did understand why he hadn't immediately shared that kind of information. It wasn't like she had led with 'Hi I'm Flick Hunter, I have one hundred and sixty-four pounds, eighty-seven pence in my account.' It had just come as such a shock. Luke didn't act or look like a millionaire. It had also been hard to hear her nan dismiss what they'd shared because he hadn't told Flick the truth.

She walked into his studio but while the lights were on and there was evidence he had been working there, he wasn't there now. She wondered, briefly, if he was hiding from her in the store cupboard at the back of the studio space before she dismissed it.

She saw movement outside and realised he was in the garden standing in front of the wonky tree. She quickly moved outside.

'Hey,' she said.

He glanced at her and then looked back to the tree.

She chewed her lip and stepped closer.

'The storm took out three out of the four supporting cables last night and one of the poles,' Luke said, gesturing to the tree.

'Oh no.'

'We need to get someone up here quickly to try to reinforce it again but honestly anything stronger than a breeze and this thing is going to go. Look.' Luke gave the tree a shove and it rocked precariously, lifting visibly out of the ground. 'Most of the roots are dead anyway and so brittle, there's nothing really left to cling to the soil.'

'Is there anything we can do in the meantime?'

'Well, we can always get a concrete lorry to come up here and pour concrete in the hole. That might stop it from falling.'

'Wouldn't that kill it?'

'I think the tree is clinging onto life by its fingernails. There are less than half the leaves we had last year and look at the state of them, brown and curling at the edges. At least if we concreted the tree in place it would preserve the landmark.'

'I'd rather pour a load of compost in the hole with a ton of plant food and hope we can save the roots, rather than admit defeat.'

A smile spread across Luke's face. 'You really do like to fight for the underdog, don't you?'

She didn't know what to say to that.

'OK, compost it is. I'll make some phone calls and see what we can do about getting the tree reinforced too.' He turned and walked away.

Flick stared after him. Were they really not going to talk about this?

She moved towards him. 'Luke, wait.'

He turned back and suddenly his eyes widened in horror and he charged towards her. He rugby tackled her to the ground, cradling her body and head as they hit the floor just as the branches of the tree landed around them with a loud crash.

Her heart was racing at what had just happened but to her relief she realised they were surrounded by the thinner branches near the top, which shouldn't have caused any injury. So she was shocked when Luke let out a moan of pain.

'Oh my god Luke, are you OK?' Flick said.

He let out another groan and a wheeze.

She moved her hands round his back to make sure he hadn't been speared by one of the branches. She checked his back, sides, shoulders, neck and bum but could find no obvious sign of injury.

'Is it your legs?' She couldn't reach those, pinned under the weight of his body.

He shook his head. 'I'm OK, just give me a sec,' he croaked.

Her heart was still racing with fear. They were surrounded by the branches of the fallen tree and she couldn't move to help him. 'Have you broken something?'

He shook his head again, still wheezing in pain. 'Are you OK?'

'Yes, where are you hurt?' She felt around his back again.

'My balls,' he groaned.

'What?'

'You kneed me in the balls when I threw you to the ground.'

'Oh my god.' She tried to rearrange her legs so she wasn't putting pressure on them. 'Are you OK?'

'I will be in a minute.'

She let out a sigh of relief. 'I should hope so, we need everything working down there for when we have more incredible sex.'

His eyebrows shot up. 'There's going to be more incredible sex?'

'There better be. You've ruined me for other men.'

A smile spread across his face but then he frowned. 'But you thought I had an ulterior motive for buying you all the gift shop stock.'

Her hands were still around him so she stroked them up his back. 'I never thought that, not for one second. You're one of the kindest, most wonderful men I've ever met and I trust you completely. And I'm sorry if I made you think otherwise. When you asked me if that's what I thought, I did have to stop and analyse whether my experience with Ryan was making me angry and defensive or whether I was just annoyed with you for not telling me and lying to me about the kitty. Turns out I'm just annoyed with you. I'm still annoyed with you and *this* doesn't change that.'

'What doesn't change that?'

'This.' She reached up and kissed him and she felt him smile against her lips as he kissed her back.

She pulled back to stroke his face. 'I am still very annoyed with you,' she said softly.

He grinned. 'I know.' He kissed her again and it made her needy and weak.

She pulled back again. 'Especially because you let me spend thousands of pounds of your money. I would never have done that if I'd known.'

'I know. But it made it easier to give it when you thought it came from a kitty, and you still fought against it, demanding to pay the kitty back.'

'I know a few thousand pounds is probably nothing to you, but it's still your money. I will be happier once all the gift shop stuff is going back.'

He shook his head. 'The gift shop stuff stays. If you want more incredible sex, you're going to have to let me have that.'

She let out a laugh of outrage. 'You can't blackmail me with sex.'

He kissed her neck, just below her ear, sending pleasure darting through her stomach. 'It's your choice really, hot sex every morning,' he kissed her again, trailing his mouth down her throat. 'Every night.' He kissed her again. 'And probably even every lunchtime. Or you return the gift shop stock.' He kissed her on her shoulder, at the bottom of her neck. 'You have to decide what's more important, your principles or an endless supply of really hot sex.'

She closed her eyes as he moved his mouth across her chest, following the V-cut of her dress. She gasped as his lips grazed her breast. 'My principles are very important to me,' she said and she was surprised by how desperate her voice sounded. 'But so is hot sex.'

'It's a tough choice.' He moved his mouth to her heart.

'I think,' she stroked a hand through his hair. 'When I'm not angry anymore, you should show me that hot sex again and then I can make an informed decision.'

'Good idea.' He pushed himself back from her, lifting the branches away from her, and then held out a hand to help her up. She took it and he pulled her to her feet and then, still holding her hand, he marched towards the house.

'Where are we going?'

'We're going to have make-up sex.'

'But I'm still annoyed with you,' Flick protested as she hurried to catch up with him. 'And now I have blackmail to add to your list of heinous crimes.'

'Then we'll have angry sex.'

She looked back over at the tree, lying completely intact on the floor. 'What about the wonky tree?'

'It'll still be there when we get back.'

She had no more words of protest as he marched through the house, up the backstairs, straight into their flat and into his bedroom. He turned her so her back was against the wall and then he kissed her.

She wrapped her arms round his neck, pressing herself up against him and she could feel how much he wanted her.

'Everything working OK down there now?' Flick asked. 'I'm not giving up my principles for faulty goods.'

'Everything is fine, you'll see for yourself in a minute.'

She undid his jeans and pushed them down around his bum and then slipped her hand inside his shorts. He was rock hard. He let out a moan as she moved her hand around him.

'Everything seems fine, but would you like me to take a closer look?'

'We'll never get to the make-up sex if you do, or if you keep touching me like that.' He took her hand from his shorts and kissed it. 'And I would much rather hear you scream than anything else.'

She smiled at that.

He kissed her again as he reached round her back and unzipped her dress, letting it fall to the floor. Without taking his mouth from hers, he removed her bra too, before filling his hands with her breasts.

She quickly wrestled him out of his t-shirt and wriggled out of her knickers, then pushed his jeans and shorts down.

He stepped out of them. 'You have zero patience.'

'Not when it comes to you.'

He smiled and kissed her again, moving his hand between her legs. His touch was perfect, knowing exactly what she needed, her body responding to him instantly, and that feeling started coiling in her stomach as if it had simply been waiting there, waiting for him.

She pressed herself up against him, desperate to feel his body against hers. She could feel herself tightening, standing on the edge, her movements getting frantic as she needed that release.

'Luke.'

'I've got you.' He bent his head and took her breast in his mouth and she shattered, falling apart so fiercely that she was thankful he was holding her up. She clung to him as waves of pleasure rode through her.

She was still shaking as she came down from her high. He kissed her on the forehead, stroking her arms and shoulders. 'You OK?'

'I'm with you, I'm definitely more than OK.'

He smiled and kissed her, as she stroked his face.

He pulled back slightly and grabbed a condom from the drawers. After a moment, he lifted her, she wrapped her arms and legs around him and he slid perfectly inside of her as if he was made just for her. His eyes were on hers the whole time as he set a slow, exquisite pace.

'You're not good at the angry sex,' she teased.

'You want me to be more ferocious?'

She stroked a thumb across his lips before giving him a sweet kiss. 'I'm not sure you have it in you.'

He gave a little growl that sounded more like a kitten purring and she let out a snort of laughter. 'Oh my god, I love you.'

He stilled, the smile falling from his face. 'What?'

Oh god, the horror of telling him she loved him the second time they were making love. Why had she said that? Did she love him? She knew she was falling for him fast and hard but this felt too soon even for her.

'I didn't mean *that*. It was more the kind of "I love you" that you might say to a friend.'

'A friend?' Luke said in surprise, which was understandable considering he was buried deep inside of her.

'Not a friend, you're much more than that, but it was a different kind of "I love you" than the "I'm in love with you" kind. It wasn't that. You don't need to worry.'

'OK. I'm not worried.' Although he was still looking at her as if he was.

'Let's just put that in the "never happened" box too.'

He let out a little sigh of relief and smiled as he started moving against her again. 'OK. But that box is getting rather full and it's only been a few days.'

She stroked his face and kissed him, trying to distract him from her faux pas, even though she felt a little bit hurt by his reaction to it. Of course he wasn't going to fall in love with her after a few days and she was silly to let her heart get so carried away. She just needed to enjoy it for what it was.

He shifted her higher and she gasped as he touched that sweet spot inside of her.

She tried really hard to concentrate on what he was doing, how wonderful it felt as he made love to her, and that feeling that was already building again in the pit of her stomach. She tried not to think about how she really needed to leave her emotions at the door when it came to Luke. He was leaving in a few weeks, she couldn't let herself fall in love with this brilliant, kind, wonderful man because it was quite likely when he left, he'd put her in the 'never happened' box too and move on with his life for good.

CHAPTER ELEVEN

By the time they'd got back downstairs, the wonky tree had amassed quite a crowd. Word had either spread very quickly or people had seen it from the town and come hurrying up here to see what had happened to their treasured landmark for themselves. The atmosphere was quite subdued, people were sad or shocked. Although the wonky tree was important to them, most of them clearly hadn't been up to see it in person or they'd have realised that it was slowly dying over the last few years and it was only the cables holding it up.

Luke did feel a little bit guilty that while people had gathered around the tree to mourn its loss, he'd been upstairs having the time of his life, but he certainly didn't regret it. It wasn't as if not having sex would have changed the outcome.

Ethel eyed them as they walked over to the tree and joined the crowd. 'Where have you two been?' she said in such a way that said she knew where they'd been and what they'd been doing and how disgusted she was by it.

Luke couldn't care less what she thought. He couldn't be happier and nothing could burst his bubble of happiness. He thought about telling Ethel he'd just had Flick pinned to the wall and again in the shower just to see her face but he didn't think Flick would appreciate that.

'We were trying to contact an arborist,' Luke said, calmly, which was partly true. He had phoned one while Flick was getting dressed.

'Why?' Aidan scoffed. 'The tree is dead.'

'The roots are still intact, we might be able to do something to save it.'

'Why?'

'Look around, Aidan. These people have come up here because the tree means something to them, it means something to the many people who have captured stunning pictures of it over the years or come up here specifically to see it. It's been here for over a hundred years, it's part of the heritage of Lovegrove Bay and while we might not be able to save the life of the tree, we should try to save the structure of it. Restore it back in its place.'

'Well, I for one will miss seeing it,' Ethel said, pulling out a tissue from her sleeve and wiping her eyes. 'Every time I drive back from London and I come over this hill towards the town, the tree is like a sign that I'm finally home.'

'I agree,' Rose said. 'It's a symbol of Lovegrove Bay.

It's on every postcard, it's used as the logo for lots of local establishments, it's not just iconic for the people of Lovegrove Bay, it's a national landmark.'

'It's also been the inspiration for a lot of art over the years, paintings, sculptures, embroidery. I've even done mosaics of it,' Katherine said.

'Well, yes, I suppose it would be a shame if it wasn't there anymore,' Aidan back-pedalled.

'If we can't save it, we can lift it back up and set it in concrete so it doesn't fall over again,' Luke said.

'But without the leaves it's not going to look particularly attractive though, is it?' Aidan said. 'It will just be a dead tree. No one is going to come and see that.'

Maybe he had a point. Although the famous shape would be preserved, without the life would it lose its appeal?

They were all silent for a moment while they thought.

'Luke could carve the trunk of the tree with patterns or pictures,' Flick said, looking at him hopefully and he smiled. He loved how hard she was fighting for this place and how she kept coming up with different ways to save it. Carving the tree was a great idea and quite honestly he would give her the world if it kept that smile on her face.

'I can do that,' Luke said, giving her hand a squeeze.

'I can embroider or quilt some leaves that we can add to it,' Ethel said.

'I could mosaic some glass beads into any of the cracks,' Katherine offered.

'I could paint some rocks to go round the base or inlaid into the concrete,' Rose said.

They all looked at Aidan to see what he would offer and he sighed. 'I could make some flowers out of clay.'

'All of that will be gorgeous additions to the tree,' Flick said. 'And will showcase the art from the studios brilliantly.'

'And if we are doing a big reopening, maybe we need to launch with a new name too,' Ethel said. 'Maybe it could be called the Wonky Tree Studios instead.'

Flick smiled. 'I like that. I'd have to check with Audrey of course, but maybe a new name would really help the relaunch.'

Luke was quite confident that it would be her passion and drive that would help the relaunch, but a new name couldn't hurt and it might help the people of the town get behind it too.

∽

Nick, the arborist, shook his head. 'Sadly I think this is beyond even my capabilities.' He ran his hand over the thinner, spindly parts of the roots. 'Ninety percent of the roots are long dead and even the best care and supplements or plant food aren't going to bring them back.'

'But these leaves have grown so there's still life in there,' Flick said, clinging to hope with her fingernails.

'A healthy tree this size would have thousands of leaves, or tens of thousands. But there's probably no more than a hundred leaves and they don't look good. They're dry, curling and turning brown long before autumn is here. Plus if there was the slightest chance the tree could be saved, which there isn't, it would need to go back in the ground now and we would need a JCB or a crane to lift it back in and that would take a few days to organise, which would be too late. The best thing I can do is take cuttings and plant them now and hope for the best. Hopefully we might have wonky saplings this time next year.'

Flick smiled at the thought of baby wonky trees.

'What about our plan to at least try and save the structure of the tree, raise it up somehow and set it in concrete? Would that work?' Luke asked.

Nick shrugged. 'It should be OK. That's not my area of expertise. But I know wooden sculptures, chainsaw carvings, things like that, have been set in concrete to stop them falling over or from being stolen so it should be fine. With my health and safety cap on, you'll need a lot more chains and supports to secure it. You don't want any visitors up here to get squashed if the supports break like they did last night.'

'No, I'm sure we can make it safer,' Luke said.

'Right, I'll crack on and get those cuttings planted. Anywhere in particular you'd like them?' Nick said.

Luke deferred to Flick.

'Umm, along the driveway would be great,' Flick said.

Nick nodded and started work.

Flick let out a sigh of disappointment. She felt sad

that the tree was dead and there was nothing they could do to save its life but it had clearly been dying for many years. But at least they could still preserve it as a landmark and with the artists' help they could bring it back to life, at least visually.

They wandered over to Ethel who was tapping away at her tablet.

'I'm just letting our followers know the latest update,' Ethel said.

Flick was surprised that she had set up a Facebook group to save the tree and in a few hours it already had seventeen thousand members. She hadn't known Ethel held such sway with the town. The tree obviously meant something to a lot of people.

'Everyone loves our idea to resurrect the tree and then bring it back to life with our art,' Ethel said. 'I've set up a GoFundMe page to raise money for a JCB and driver or a crane. Hopefully a JCB would be enough to lift it. I've asked a company to come up here and quote for it and see if it's something they could do. If not it will have to be a crane which will be somewhere between eight and ten thousand pounds. But if everyone in the group donates a pound, we'll easily have enough money for that. We'll also need a concrete lorry with enough concrete to fill that hole and support the tree so that will come out of the funds raised too.'

'Wow, thanks for doing that, Ethel,' Luke said.

'You don't have to thank me. Enough people in this town see you as a cash cow, why should you pay for everything?' She gave Flick a glare, obviously not impressed with Flick inadvertently letting Luke pay for her gift shop, and Flick shifted uneasily. 'And you're leaving, the tree isn't going to benefit you in any way. If they want to save the tree then they need to put their hands in their pockets.'

Luke was clearly surprised by this attitude. He cleared his throat. 'I want to save the tree as much as anyone else. I'm happy to contribute.'

'One pound, you'll pay the same as everyone else,' Ethel said.

Luke nodded. 'OK.'

'Right, I've got some calls to make,' Ethel said, and walked off before they could say another word.

'Well, it's nice to see Ethel finally rally behind something, even if it is just the tree and not the studios itself,' Flick said.

'Who knew it would take a storm and the tree falling down to get her to do it.'

'Now we just need to figure out what it will take to get Aidan on our side.'

'That might take a small miracle,' Luke said. 'Fancy a walk?'

'Yes, that would be lovely.'

He took her hand and they started walking along the clifftop coastal path that went straight past the house. The sky was already starting to turn a candyfloss pink painting the town below them in a rosy glow. It looked beautiful. Out in the bay, Flick could see dolphins playing and jumping through the waves. She would never get tired of watching them or looking at that view.

They were quiet as they walked along and Flick couldn't stop thinking about Ethel's comment about everyone seeing Luke as a cash cow and her glare that inferred that Flick was clearly as bad as everyone else.

'You're thinking about what Ethel said, aren't you?'

She smiled. 'How did you know?'

'I can feel it when you're worried. You go all quiet and inside yourself.'

She loved that he knew her so well already. 'A lot of people will assume I'm only with you for your money.'

'I know. Natalia has already told me that you're a gold digger and she heard you plotting to get my money.'

'What?' Flick was outraged.

'Well, it was quite obvious she wasn't going to politely take a step back when she has been so relentless in her pursuit of me. She was obviously going to try devious means to get me to dump you and go out with her instead.'

'Why are you so blasé about this?'

'I know it's hurtful, but people will think what they want to think and there isn't a lot we can do about that. Sadly, most people will see us together and assume the only reason you're with me is because of my money rather than because of any of my qualities.'

Her heart broke for him. She could live with people thinking she was a gold digger, if that was what they wanted to believe. At least she knew the truth. But for

Luke it was worse, another dent in his confidence. Because if they believed that, it meant they didn't believe that Luke would be able to get a woman without his cash. And she wondered if that would make him start to believe that too and doubt what they had.

'I'm not with you for your money.'

'I know.'

'I don't know how to prove that to you but I'm not.'

'I know.'

'I mean, how could I have been plotting to get your money? I didn't know you were rich. How would I have known? Millionaires normally live in fancy houses with swimming pools and flashy cars, you live in a tiny two-bedroom flat with my nan.'

'I don't need or want those things. Being rich means I can spend my days wood carving which I love instead of commuting to a job I hate, it means I never have to worry about paying a bill or where my next meal is coming from. That's all I need to be content in my life. And I'm living with your nan because she needed the rent money and because she was lonely. We got on well, she makes the best chicken pie in the world, it seemed like the obvious solution.'

She smiled. 'You moved in with my nan because of her chicken pie?' There was something so sweet and endearing about that.

'Have you tried her chicken pie?'

'I can't say I have.'

'When you've eaten her pie, then you'll understand.'

She wasn't sure any pie would be that good someone

would prefer to live in a small two-bedroom flat with a flatmate over living in a luxury house, but Luke had clearly moved in for her nan, not for him and she loved him a little bit more for that.

'And I know you're not with me for my money.'

She paused. 'How do you know?'

He stopped and turned to face her, stroking a hair off her cheek. 'Because whenever something goes wrong for the people of Lovegrove Bay, a broken-down car, a broken roof, a school that needs a new nursery, everyone looks to me expecting to me to pay out, which I do, and not one of them has ever offered to pay me back like you did. You didn't even know about my money until this morning and your reaction to finding out was real, I could tell that. And because you're the kindest, loveliest, most genuine person I've ever met and I trust you not to be some scheming little minx. But most importantly I could see it in your eyes when we made love, you looked at me like I was somebody special, like I meant something to you. It's been a long time since anyone looked at me like that. I know what we have is something real, that you like me for me, not how much I have in my bank.'

She smiled with relief. It didn't matter what anyone thought as long as they both knew the truth. She looped her arms around his neck and kissed him. 'I like you very much, for many, many reasons but mainly because you really are a god of sex.'

Luke laughed loudly.

She stroked his face. 'This is real for me too. I know

this is very new for us and you're moving to Scotland and I'm starting a life here and I have no idea what will happen in a few weeks – I suppose you might be bored of me by then. But right now, being with you is absolutely my favourite way to spend my time.'

He smiled. 'For me too. So can we please stop worrying about what other people think? If we're happy that's all that matters.'

'I agree.'

'Good, now let's go. If we carry on down the coast a little way we'll come to Minack Theatre which has always reminded me of Lothlorien in *Lord of the Rings*.'

She smiled. She loved his geekiness. In fact there was a lot she loved about Luke Donnelly.

∽

Luke was lying on the sofa that night with Flick cuddled up on top of his chest as they watched the first film in *The Lord of the Rings* trilogy. He loved that he could do this with her, not one of his girlfriends had ever been interested in Lord of the Rings or any of the fantasy books he loved.

They'd just got to the part where Arwen gives Aragorn the Evenstar necklace as a symbol of her enduring love and her commitment to give up her immortality to be with him.

'I love this part of the films,' Flick said. 'It wasn't really mentioned in the books but my romantic heart adores their love story in the films. This line here where she says that she would rather live one life with him than live forever without him is just beautiful.'

'It's a big romantic gesture. I'm not sure any woman would ever love me that much.'

'Not too many women are immortal sadly.'

He laughed. 'No, I mean that epic, "I would die for you" kind of love. Do you think love is ever really like that? That big, fill-your-heart-to-the-top, last-forever kind of love?'

'I hope so. Isn't that what any love story should have? If you're going to marry someone, stand up in front of a room full of people and say this is the person you want to spend the rest of your life with, it has to be a big kind of love.'

'Ever had it?' Luke asked, stroking her hair.

She looked up at him, resting her chin on his chest as she stared at him and it filled him with hope. Was she thinking that she felt that way for him?

'No,' she said as if choosing her words carefully. 'I don't think any past relationship has ever given me that. I thought I was in love a few times, but looking back I don't think it was ever that all-consuming, can't-eat, can't-sleep, can't-breathe kind of love.'

'Me neither. I loved Sophie but it wasn't an everlasting type of love. And with Martine I think it was an infatuation not love. I could never see marriage and a happy ever after with either of them.'

Flick was still studying him as if seeing something she hadn't expected. 'Maybe one day we'll find that.'

He stroked her hair. 'I hope one day you do, you deserve someone incredible.'

She smiled at him. 'Oh Luke, I hope one day when you fall in love, you find someone who realises how utterly amazing you are.'

He kissed her on the forehead and turned his attention back to the film. His feelings for her were growing deeper every day; he didn't think it would be long before he was head over heels in love with her, no matter how hard he tried to hold himself back. He only hoped that when he got there, she felt the same way too. He couldn't help thinking what she'd said that morning when they were making love, when she'd inadvertently said she loved him. She said she loved him like a friend, before she quickly back-pedalled away from that. If he fell in love with her and she told him she only saw him as a friend, just like Sophie had, that would destroy him.

CHAPTER TWELVE

Luke was pacing nervously round his studio the next day as he prepared for their first workshop. He'd had a few calls with an art therapist from Headway, a brain injury charity, and she'd talked about various ways he and the other artists could meet the needs of the people attending the workshops. A lot of it was considering accessibility as some people's brain injuries meant they could no longer walk, like Frank today, but the workshops were going to take place on the ground floor and the double doors at the front were big enough to accommodate a wheelchair. They had a disabled toilet on the ground floor too. From the artists' point of view it was about offering the attendees a choice of ways to express themselves with multiple mediums. Woodwork was a tricky one because it required using a range of tools and Luke just wanted to make sure that anyone doing one of his workshops could use the tools safely.

As they were just starting the workshops at the

studios, they only had one person coming today to take part: Frank, who had slipped on some ice in the winter and smacked his head on the floor. Since then it had been many months of recovery and rehabilitation. He was coming with his husband Daniel.

A small van pulled up outside and Luke looked at Flick nervously.

'You'll be great. I can't think of a better person for this. You're the kindest person I've ever met. You'll be perfect at this.'

He smiled at that. She had such faith in him.

A man, presumably Daniel, got out and came through the front door.

'Hi, are you here for the workshop?' Flick asked.

'Yes, hi, I'm Daniel, Frank is in the van. I just wanted to have a quick chat about him before we start. He can't walk or talk but he can understand everything you say and can communicate in other ways. We're both learning sign language and he has one of those electronic talk pads where he presses the buttons to say the words he wants but he doesn't really like using that as it takes so much time to write out a sentence. He can still use his hands though sometimes they get a bit shaky.'

Daniel let out a sigh as he looked out to the van. 'He is... frustrated and angry. And understandably so. He was so fit and active before the accident. Six months ago, we'd go out hiking over the hills for miles every day. We'd swim in the sea and now he can't do those things and he's angry about it. Just one tiny little accident that should have left him with a few cuts and bruises and it ruined his life. He doesn't want to be here today. He thinks workshops for those with brain injuries are patronising. But he loved woodwork prior to the accident. He was always busy making things, a treasure chest for our granddaughter, a jewellery box with little drawers that would slide out and secret compartments, a dressing-up box, he loved wood-turning bowls and other things. And he absolutely loved teaching our grandchildren how to do it. He'd teach them how to measure, how to cut and use the other tools and how to put them all together to make a sailboat or a pencil box or a money box. But we had a big workshop in our garden and since the accident we've had to move to a new place that is all on the ground floor with wider doors and ramps for a wheelchair. The new place doesn't have a garden let alone room for a workshop or shed so he's not been able to do any of that and I think he misses it. So I thought today would be good for him.'

'It sounds like this might be exactly what he needs,' Flick said.

'I'll go and get him and I apologise now if he's rude to you.'

'You don't need to worry, we understand how frustrating this must be for him,' Luke said.

Daniel disappeared back out the front door and Luke looked around his studio. What he'd planned to do with Frank went straight out the window for fear of it being too simple or patronising. This was a man who knew his way around a woodwork studio, who knew the tools and the machines. He'd been going to suggest he carve a leaf out of wood or whittle a small animal like a bird or fish and then paint it afterwards but that was way too simplistic. He was going to have to adapt.

He looked out the window and saw Daniel wheeling Frank towards the front door and he hurried over to open the door for them. He could tell straightaway that Frank was annoyed about being here. It was one of the things that the lady from Headway talked about, that some people with acquired brain injuries really struggled with their new normal. Some people just adapted, they persevered, they found ways to enjoy and live their lives with their body's restrictions or disabilities. Those who had lost the use of their hands might paint with their mouth or feet for example. Those who had lost their short-term memory, so might forget instructions as soon as they were given or what was happening in a book they were reading, would make notes as they read so they could still enjoy the pleasure of reading even if it took them longer. And she said there were those who didn't want to adapt, who mourned their old lives and didn't want to change. She said, especially in the first year, there was a grieving process and they had to find a way to work their way through it. Frank was clearly in the latter category and understandably so. Luke didn't know what he would do if he suddenly lost the ability to talk or walk or carve wood. Wood carving was his favourite thing in the world.

Luke held out his hand. 'Hi Frank, I'm Luke and this is Flick.'

Frank rolled his eyes and reluctantly shook Luke's hand and then Flick's.

'Pleased to meet you,' Flick said.

Daniel wheeled him into Luke's workshop and Frank looked around. Luke saw the tiny spark in his eyes as he looked at the tools and machines.

'So Frank, I wonder if you might be able to help me,' Luke said, thinking on his feet. 'I'm a wood carver. I started off whittling very simple animals and I then progressed to the kind of sculptures you can see around the workshop. But despite working with wood every day, I've never done any of the kind of woodwork that you've done – making jewellery boxes or treasure chests or sailboats – and I hear that kind of thing is right up your street. So I was going to suggest that we can whittle some animals today, which we can absolutely do if you wish, but I thought you might want to help me build some birdboxes for future workshops. There will be people coming here who have never done any kind of woodwork before and painting and decorating birdboxes will be the extent of what they want to do. Others might want to make them but I need to know how to do that before I can teach them. So if you can teach me and we can make a few today ready to paint in future workshops then I can teach others how to make them too.'

Frank scowled and Luke wondered if he could see right through what he was trying to do. He started tapping away at his touchpad, obviously wanting to say something. After a few moments, the touchpad spoke for him and Luke was surprised to hear that the voice sounded human and not some computerised robotic voice.

'The youth of today need to learn more practical skills, it's a dying art. When I was a boy, everyone learned this kind of thing, now the youth only care about their mobile phones.'

'I totally agree,' Luke said. 'I've been teaching myself how to use the lathe lately. The results are OK, but nothing brilliant. Maybe another day you can teach me how to do that too.'

Frank nodded and then pointed to a pile of wooden planks and leftovers in the corner. Daniel wheeled him over there and Luke followed. Frank pointed at various pieces and Luke pulled them out of the pile. Frank gestured to Daniel to wheel him over to the table and Luke placed the pieces of wood down on it and quickly gathered a pencil, ruler and a few tools. Frank started drawing out the shape of the birdhouse as confidently as if he'd made hundreds of them before. He didn't falter as he picked up the little handsaw and started cutting. Luke glanced at Daniel and he mouthed, 'Thank you.'

~

Flick smiled as Frank gathered up one of the birdhouses he'd made and placed it lovingly on his lap ready to leave. He and Daniel had been here for hours, much longer than the designated workshop time, but she hadn't wanted to stop him when he was clearly enjoying himself so much. Between Frank and

Luke they had made twelve birdhouses ready for painting in another workshop and they were beautiful, with little windows, scalloped eaves and even chimneys.

Frank had come to life as he started building the birdboxes. Daniel said it was the first time he'd seen him smile since the accident and Flick loved that they had been able to help him in this way.

Luke had played his part well. She was pretty sure he would be able to build a birdbox on his own but he studiously watched Frank and copied his every move, asking questions now and again, and she could see that Frank really enjoyed helping and teaching him.

'Thank you so much,' Daniel said as he started wheeling Frank towards the door. 'This has been wonderful.'

'I've really enjoyed it too,' Luke said. 'And now we have all these perfect birdboxes ready for out next workshop. Although to be honest, I think Frank should come along and help me teach it.'

Frank nodded and then did a hand gesture.

'He wants to know how much you'll pay him,' Daniel winked.

Luke laughed and Frank joined in too.

'And if you wanted to come up here, anytime, to work on your own projects, you'd be very welcome,' Luke said, which Flick thought was a bit odd as he'd be gone in a few weeks.

Frank nodded with a big smile on his face and shook Luke's hand enthusiastically. And then they left, Daniel thanking them on the way out and the door closing behind them.

Flick moved over to Luke and wrapped her arms around him. 'That was brilliant, *you* were brilliant.'

'Thank you, I'm just glad we found something he enjoyed doing.'

'The birdboxes were a great idea. But you're not going to be here if he comes back again.'

'Well maybe I'll have to pop down to see him.' Luke cupped her face and kissed her. 'And you.'

Flick smiled at that and kissed him back. Watching Luke be so patient and kind and lovely with Frank had made her fall in love with him that much more. She had kept telling herself that it was too soon to fall in love, that she was falling for him but she wasn't there yet, but she knew that was a lie. She had already fallen, she was completely and utterly in love with him. People often likened that moment when they knew they were in love to being hit by a bus, but it hadn't been that way for her. It had been like a flower growing. Every day, every smile, every touch, every time Luke did something nice, every time he made her laugh, she had fallen for him that little bit more. There was no thunderbolt moment when she realised, for her it felt like that love had always been there, growing stronger every day.

There was the sound of someone clearing their throat behind them and they turned to see Aidan standing there.

'Sorry to interrupt but I… I've been watching you all morning and I…' he shook his head and looked away.

Flick eyed Luke in confusion. 'Frank is my dad. We don't speak anymore. It was a stupid argument six years ago and we haven't spoken since. I've tried a few times to extend the olive branch and he doesn't want to know. Silly stubborn old fool. After the accident, I came round to see if I could help and he told me he doesn't need my help and... well here we are, still not speaking. Families are hard work,' he sighed. 'I've obviously stayed in touch with Daniel without my dad knowing, to keep up to date with how he's doing, and it hurts to see him so angry and upset with the world and his predicament. I've been watching him all morning, standing over there in the shadows where he couldn't see me, and... You made him smile and, judging from what Daniel said, he hasn't had anything to smile about for a very long time. So thank you.'

'It was my pleasure,' Luke said.

'I was against the idea of teaching workshops because, quite honestly, I don't like people and I thought teaching them would piss me off. I'm not a patient man and I just like to be left alone to do my pottery and not have to deal with customers or students. But what you are doing here is of vital importance. It means something to them, I can see that. Watching my dad this morning, he came alive. This is why we have to save the studios, for them. So I'm all in, whatever it takes. I'm not saying I'd be any good at teaching workshops, but perhaps if you were there, Flick, to add the kindness factor we could muddle through. I'll produce smaller items to sell in my workshop, I'll do demonstrations, I'll put together pottery take-home kits for people to try their hand at pottery in their own homes, I'll make flowers for the wonky tree, I'll… ride a horse naked through town promoting our studio, if that's what it takes. Because this matters. And I just wanted to say I'm behind you now, one hundred percent.'

Flick blinked in surprise. 'Thank you. Although I don't think nudity is required.'

'Thank god,' Aidan muttered.

'I think pottery would be a wonderful activity to offer those with brain injuries,' Flick said. 'But I certainly don't want you to do something you're not comfortable with. Perhaps we could get a pottery teacher to come up here and run a workshop, maybe from your studio and you could be there to help, if needed?'

'I like the sound of that.'

'But thank you for your support.'

Aidan nodded and walked away and Flick couldn't help but smile that they'd finally found something to make him care.

∽

Flick walked into the café a while later ready for Polly's soft launch. She was doing a small taste testing first for the artists before the people of the town would arrive.

Quinn and Alex had been busy all morning moving into their studio spaces which were next door to each other. Flick and Luke had been helping them for a little while after the workshop had finished but it was quite clear Alex had wanted the space to make the studio her own so they'd left them to it and Flick had spent a few hours putting the finishing touches on her gift shop instead. It wasn't quite ready to open yet, but if people from the taste testing wandered in this afternoon and had a look around, that wouldn't be a bad thing.

All the artists, including Quinn and Alex, were there in the café sitting around a large table, as Polly ferried drinks over to them. Flick sat down next to Luke and took his hand. He smiled at her.

'What drink can I get you?' Polly asked Flick.

'Oh, just a tea will be fine, thanks.'

Polly hurried back off to the kitchen and Flick looked around at the finished mural. Little bees danced over the walls, flitting between brightly coloured flowers and emerald stalks of grass. It looked wonderful.

'Rose, this looks amazing,' Flick said.

Rose beamed with pride. 'Thank you.'

'People coming here are going to love it, it really brightens up the place.'

Polly came over with a tea. 'I love it, I can't stop looking at it. You've definitely earned your free cake for the next month, Rose.' She placed the mug down in front of Flick. 'So in front of you we have upside-down pineapple cake, banana and chocolate chip cake, coffee and walnut, orange and lemon cake, a variation on Eve's pudding which is basically apple cake and a triple chocolate cake. If you want to take a slice and tell me what you think, that would be great.'

'Just one slice?' Ethel said.

'You can have as many slices as you like,' Polly said. 'As long as you eat them and they don't go to waste. I've made a few more of the same that are out the back for when the villagers come up here so hopefully we won't run out.'

'Maybe a very thin slice of each,' Rose said.

'That's a good idea,' Aidan said.

They all tucked into various flavours of cakes and noises of appreciation could be heard from everyone.

'This apple cake is heaven,' Flick said.

'I could die happy eating this chocolate cake,' Luke said.

There were other comments and groans of joy as they polished off their thin slices and went back for seconds.

Polly let out a small sigh of relief. 'Cakes aren't really my speciality so I was hoping they'd be OK.'

'Better than OK,' Ethel said.

'Any feedback?'

'More please,' Aidan said, helping himself to a third slice.

They all laughed.

'I'm not sure I like the jam on the chocolate cake,' Rose said. 'But that's a personal preference, there's nothing wrong with it.'

'No, that's fair,' Polly said.

'I think the orange and lemon cake needs orange and

lemon buttercream in the middle not vanilla, but the cake itself is moist and delicious,' Katherine said.

'OK, I can do that. Any other suggestions?' Polly looked around the table.

There was silence for a moment, then Alex spoke. 'I think they're delicious. Far better than anything I could ever do.'

Polly smiled. 'Right, I'm going to get ready for all the villagers. Please do help yourselves to more cake.'

She hurried off to the kitchen.

'So I have some news,' Ethel said. 'There's a JCB and a concrete lorry coming tomorrow. We've raised the funds we need very quickly and, fortunately, my son knows someone who hires out JCBs and I've had a chat with them and they think they can do it. So the tree will be raised back into its original position and concreted in and then we can start decorating it. Alex and Quinn, do you have something you'd like to add to the tree?'

'I think you definitely need a few monsters, lurking in the branches,' Quinn said.

'I can donate a few baubles but I'm not sure how well they will stand up to our British weather.'

'I've thought about that,' Ethel said. 'Anything we hang on the tree like leaves, flowers or other decorations could be changed every few months so we have seasonal decorations: eggs, chicks and rabbits at Easter; Halloween decorations in October; maybe even pirate decorations next year for our next pirate festival,' Ethel said.'

'That's a good idea,' Rose said. 'That would be an

attraction, people would come up here to see the new decorations.'

'Also our followers love that the studios are going to be renamed the Wonky Tree Studios,' Ethel went on. 'Lots of people are very supportive of the workshops we are doing here for those with brain injuries and some people have volunteered their time to come and help us smarten up the place ready for the reopening. Some people are going to tidy up the garden for us tomorrow and some are going to help paint the front of the house.'

'That's wonderful,' Flick said. 'Will everyone be ready if we do the grand opening on Sunday? I know there are still some areas of the house that need touching up or renovating but I think we can still do the launch and work on those things later. It would be good to capitalise on the extra footfall in the town this weekend because of the pirate festival.'

Everyone nodded.

Flick looked over at Polly and she nodded too. 'My new countertops are being delivered tomorrow morning. Ben can fit them for me tomorrow afternoon. After that I'm ready to go.'

'OK, I'll get the word out,' Flick said, making a note to work on some Facebook and Instagram ads and posts on local forums that afternoon.

They talked between themselves for a few minutes then Katherine cleared her throat. 'So what's happening between you two?' she asked Luke and Flick.

'Oh yes.' Quinn looked like all his Christmases had come at once. 'Do tell.'

Luke dropped Flick's hand. 'There's not really a lot to tell.'

Flick busied herself with a few crumbs on her plate. While she recognised that Luke was trying to protect what they had and not turn their relationship into a source of gossip, it still hurt a little to hear him dismiss it.

'So it's just casual sex?' Ethel said, pulling a face.

'It's very new right now,' Flick said.

'But aren't you leaving in a week or two?' Ethel said to Luke.

'Yes,' Luke said. 'I officially get the keys on Monday. And then there's a few weeks of renovations before I can move in.'

There was no hesitation, no explanation, nothing to say that he might stay if things worked out between them.

'So you'll just sleep with him, get what you want from him and then he leaves?' Ethel said.

'Ethel,' Luke's voice was firm. 'Flick is not with me for my money. As hard as it is to believe, she actually likes me for me. And whether you believe that or not, I don't care. I trust her completely.'

'Sorry.' Ethel looked suitably chastised. 'I'm just looking out for you, that's all.'

'Well I don't need it, especially not when the things you say are clearly hurtful to us both.'

There was an awkward silence.

'Yeah, sorry,' Quinn said. 'I like to wind Luke up because he's my mate and that's what we do, but it wasn't my intention to hurt you, Flick. He is ridiculously happy with you, that's good enough for me.'

Alex stood up. 'This whole conversation is making me feel uncomfortable, I feel like I'm back at school. I'm going back to work, there's a lot to do to my studio before the grand opening on Sunday.'

'I'll give you a hand,' Quinn said, flashing Flick an apologetic smile as he hurried out the room after Alex.

'I'm going back to work on the gift shop,' Flick said, she stood up and walked out the room.

～

'Are you OK?'

Flick looked up from where she was adding fairy lights to some of the shelves to see Luke leaning against the doorway.

'Yeah.'

'It doesn't matter what they think, remember.'

'I know, it's just hard to hear. Though I do appreciate you sticking up for me.'

He moved closer.

'And I'm sorry for downplaying what we have. I wasn't expecting Katherine or anyone to start asking about us. I didn't know what to say. Our relationship is private and, while I have no intention of hiding it, I'm certainly not going to tell everyone that you straddling me as we made love this morning was the single sexiest thing I've ever seen.'

She smiled and not just at the memory of him lying in his bed, staring up at her as if she was a goddess.

'It's OK, I don't want to share that kind of stuff either. I guess no one will really take us seriously because you're leaving in a few weeks.'

'Yeah, I know.'

And that was it, he didn't say anything else. No offers to stay, no, 'We'll cross that bridge when we come to it.' It was hard for her to take what they had seriously, let alone anyone else. She wanted to talk to him about it but she supposed it was too early for big discussions about their future. She had a few more weeks yet. She ignored the voice in the back of her head that said in a few weeks she would be head over heels in love and if he left he would break her heart.

'Are you coming to the pirate festival on Saturday?' Luke asked, which was a change of subject if ever she heard one.

'Yeah, it sounds like fun.'

'Are you going to dress up?'

'Oh sure. I can pop down to the costume shop tomorrow afternoon.'

'They might be a bit lacking in pirate outfits by now, people hire them out weeks or months in advance, but I'm sure they can find you something suitable.'

'Have you already hired out yours?'

'I have my own, in fact a lot of people do, so you might still be able to get one from the costume shop.'

'I love that you have your own. My sexy Captain Blackbeard,' she said, looping her arms round his neck.

Just then she heard a cough coming from the door that led to the café. She looked up to see a woman standing there and quickly let go of Luke.

'Hello?'

'Hi, sorry to disturb you. I was just next-door having coffee and cake and I thought I'd have a nose around. Is this a gift shop?'

'Yes it is,' Flick said. 'We're not strictly open right now, but—'

'But we're doing a preview event today and over the weekend,' Luke said.

'That's right,' Flick said. 'So feel free to have a look around.'

'We have craft kits down here, everything you would need to have a go at pretty much any arts or craft that you can think of,' Luke gestured around the room. 'Upstairs we have the regular gifts like scarves and mugs and chocolate.'

'Great, thank you.'

'Take your time and give us a shout if you need anything.'

The woman moved off and Luke gave Flick an excited thumbs up. 'Your first customer.'

'Hello, are you open?' came another voice from the door. Flick looked over to see a couple standing at the door.

'Yes, please do come in and have a look,' Flick said excitedly. She turned to Luke. 'You better get back to your own studio, just in case you have any customers in there.'

He nodded, gave her a quick kiss on the cheek and hurried from the room. She watched the people walk around the room, picking up the craft kits and clearly thinking about the possibilities they could create themselves. It was exciting to think she might be starting someone off on a new hobby or passion for art today and she couldn't help smiling about that.

∽

Luke had just finished displaying his sculptures around the shop. He hadn't had enough time to do as many as he'd have liked but there were enough to showcase his work.

He looked up to see Flick wandering in with a big smile on her face. She walked up and slid her arms around him, giving him a big hug.

'Hey, how did it go at your impromptu preview event?' Luke asked, stroking her back.

She looked up at him and smiled. 'It was great. I wasn't expecting so many people but I've easily had forty people come in and have a look around. And people were buying things, a lot bought the standard gifts and that's fine, I feel happy that I chose stuff that appeals to people. But the majority of people were buying arts and craft kits, the mosaic ones especially were popular, as were the little wood-whittling kits. It made me so happy to think of people going home and making the time to be crafty and that I helped them to do it. Doing arts and crafts is such a positive thing, for so many reasons. So many people say they don't have the time or the skill so selling little kits with all the instructions and materials they need might give them the inspiration to make time and learn a new skill. And a few people bought the kits as gifts for other people. What a lovely gift to pass on to someone else.'

He smiled at her excitement and enthusiasm. 'I'm so pleased. We even had people coming in here. I sold three smaller sculptures and someone has asked for a commission for a medium-sized piece.'

'That's great, I knew once we got people through the door then sales would increase, especially if we offered smaller, cheaper items alongside the bigger stuff. Honestly, I'm so happy, I really think this is going to be a success and it's all thanks to you.'

'Oh no, I can't take any of the credit, this is all you, your passion, your enthusiasm, your determination for it to succeed.'

'And your donation. We couldn't have done it without you. None of this would have been possible without financial help.' Flick fished in her pocket and pulled out an envelope which she handed to him.

'What's this?'

'Twenty-five percent of what I made today.'

'Oh hell no.'

'Yes, I promised to pay you back and I will.'

'No, you earned this. And we have a deal with Polly that she doesn't pay us anything for two months so she can use the money to order stock and get the business going. The same thing stands for you.'

'No, this isn't right.'

'It's my money and I can spend it however I want. I want this to work and the café and the gift shop are a huge important part of that. Use the money to buy new stock or treat yourself to a sexy pirate costume for Saturday.'

She smiled and hugged him. 'Thank you.'

'You're very welcome.'

'I will pay you back.'

'I know.'

'I just feel so happy right now. This is a new start for me, living here, working in my own gift shop. I didn't know what I was going to do with my life when I came down here and now I feel like I've found where I belong.'

Luke smiled and kissed her forehead. He was happy he could do that for her but he couldn't help feeling desperately sad that in a few weeks she might be embracing this new start without him.

CHAPTER THIRTEEN

Flick watched the wonky tree as it was finally hauled back into its rightful place the next day. It had taken a while to get the ropes in the right place for the JCB to pull it back to an upright position. Several men from the town had helped with ropes and chains around different parts of the tree. They had to be careful so as not to break any branches in the process and there had been more supporting cables attached and bolted into the ground. Once they were done pouring concrete around the roots, the tree wouldn't be going anywhere.

Flick smirked that Ethel was doing a Facebook live to all the tree's followers showing the progress and just how their money was being spent. The tree had a lot more followers than the studios, although Audrey had barely posted on any kind of social media, something Flick was determined would change once they were open.

Several of the tree's followers were busily tidying

up the garden and painting the outside of the house and it already looked a million times better than it did before.

As it was going to be a while until they were completely finished with the tree and the concrete was dry enough to get near it and decorate it, Flick decided to go down to the town and see about getting a pirate costume for the festival the next day.

The sun was shining brightly as she walked down the hill towards the harbour and beach and lots of people were sitting on benches or on the grass eating ice creams. There was a large English setter puppy running around inside a fountain, splashing about, smile on his face, clearly having the time of his life as its stressed-out owner was trying to catch it. Children were chasing each other with water pistols, there was even a yoga class taking place on the village green.

All the brightly coloured houses and shops were decorated for the pirate festival, some with hundreds of parrots, some with skeletons, some just with pirate flags. The town looked great.

She opened the door to the costume shop and stepped inside. This place was huge, there were rails and rails stuffed with every costume imaginable. Every superhero, every character from all the popular films and TV shows, every animal you could think of. She could go as an astronaut, Superman, an elephant or a block of cheese if she wanted. But the one thing she couldn't see was any pirate costumes.

A man came hurrying out of the back, carrying what

looked like Cleopatra's famous black wig. 'Oh hello, can I help you?'

'Yes, I was looking for something to wear to pirate day?'

'Oh no, we are fresh out of pirate gear. All those were reserved weeks ago. I tell people every year to book ahead, and every year I get people turn up the day before hoping to get a pirate costume only to be disappointed.'

'Yeah, Luke said that might be the case. I only arrived here a week ago so I didn't know about the pirate festival.'

'Not to worry, we'll find you something suitable,' the man said, putting the wig down carefully on a mannequin's head that was sitting near the till. 'How about a zombie? Lots of people go as ghost pirates so a zombie wouldn't be too far removed from that.'

'Mmm, that wasn't really what I was looking for.'

'Right, OK, although beggars can't be choosers.'

'No, maybe I can have a look around to see if anything inspires me.'

'Knock yourself out,' the man said, disappearing out the back.

Flick started walking around, flicking through the different outfits to see if anything was remotely suitable. She could go as a witch or an elf or a goblin, a policewoman, a fire fighter, a pilot… The possibilities were endless but none of them seemed appropriate.

Then suddenly she saw it. She pulled it out and

looked at it and couldn't help but smile. Luke was going to love this.

~

Flick walked back out to the wonky tree after stowing her costume safely in her bedroom. The tree looked great back in its rightful spot.

Rose had already set her painted stones into the concrete, depicting images of leaves and flowers intermingled with stones painted with various arts and crafts. It was the perfect symbol of Wonky Tree Studios.

Luke was already carving patterns and pictures in the tree when Flick arrived and Katherine was adding tiny squares of glass and tile into the cracks, making it look like there was a forgotten mosaic peeping out from inside the tree. Alex, Quinn, Ethel and Aidan were already hanging decorations onto the tree's branches in various mediums. Aidan's had clay leaves and flowers, Ethel had embroidered hers, Alex had made hers out of paper and put them inside plastic baubles, while Quinn was attaching little monsters made from cutlery to the branches with cable ties.

Flick had made some of her own baubles using her dandelion wishes and toadstools to make it look whimsical.

'Hey,' Flick said as she moved next to Luke.

He smiled as he looked up from carving a beautiful vine on the side of the tree. He gave her a kiss on her cheek. 'Hi, did you get a costume?'

'Oh yes.'

'What did you get?' he lowered his voice. 'Is it sexy?'

'Oh definitely, you are going to want to ravish me as soon as you see it,' she said, quietly.

His eyes lit up. 'I look forward to seeing it.'

They all worked quietly for a while, adding their own decorations to the tree. Even Polly came out and tied a couple of teacups on too, ones with leaves and floral patterns that she'd picked up at a charity shop in town. It was lovely to just all work peacefully alongside each other, no animosity, simply working together to support the studio. Finally it was done – well, apart from Luke's carvings; they would probably take a little longer. They stepped back to admire their work.

'This is wonderful,' Alex said.

Flick nodded. 'It really is.'

'Dare I say it, better than the original tree,' Ethel said, taking photos for the tree's followers.

'Well, I just want to say thank you to everyone for getting involved with this,' Flick said. 'And while I know change is difficult, thank you for embracing it and being willing to make smaller items alongside your normal pieces of art. Hopefully you'll start to see some regular sales.'

'We've already had a few,' Katherine said. 'All of us had visitors on the day Polly ran her taste testing and we all made sales. Mostly the smaller items but Rose sold one of her original paintings.'

'That's wonderful. I'm so pleased for you all. I know

the smaller items don't bring in a lot of money but it will all add up over time.'

'Twenty pounds is better than zero,' Luke said.

'In reality, we're not doing this for the money, although a bit extra is nice,' Aidan said. 'We're doing this to help hold workshops for those with brain injuries. Some things are worth fighting for.'

Flick smiled at that, they were finally a team.

CHAPTER FOURTEEN

Luke was sitting in the lounge waiting for Flick to come out of her room in her pirate costume the next day. He was already dressed ready to go. Flick was really excited for him to see her costume. He wondered what it would be like. Some of the women's pirate outfits were very sexy and revealing, with corsets, short skirts, plunging necklines. And while he would certainly appreciate that, he just hoped she'd found something she was comfortable in.

Flick opened the door a crack. 'Are you ready?'

'Yes, I'm sitting here with bated breath.'

'Try to control yourself when you see me because you're going to want to carry me off to the bedroom and have your wicked way with me.'

'I promise to restrain myself.'

She opened the door and stepped out into the lounge with the biggest smile on her face. He stared at her, the smile growing on his own face. Flick was dressed as a giant pink fluffy octopus. She had a large bulbous head with massive googly eyes and eight curly tentacles that stretched down to the floor like a very bizarre dreadlock wig.

He felt an ache in his chest and he couldn't stop smiling at her.

'I'm a kraken,' Flick said, referring to the mythical giant octopus that would consume entire boats or drag them down to the sea floor. It was a legend among sailors, fishermen and of course pirates.

Luke cleared his throat, trying to form the words because the ache in his chest was spreading. 'Yeah, you look terrifying.'

She moved towards him, tentacles outstretched in what he presumed was supposed to be a scary way. 'Do you want to ravish me?'

'Always.'

But the funny thing was, he did. Not because she looked sexy, there was nothing sexy about a giant fluffy pink octopus with an oversized head. He wanted to take her to bed because he was head over heels in love with this brilliant and incredible woman and for some reason it had taken this ridiculous octopus to make him realise it.

～

The pirate festival was a huge success. There were literally thousands of pirates walking the streets and sitting on the village green, listening to sea shanties, drinking rum, and generally enjoying much merriment. There was an old Spanish galleon docked in the harbour that looked like it was from the 1500s and ready to circumnavigate the world with Drake or Columbus at the wheel. There had been staged skirmishes on it and around it all day with pirates fighting, cannons firing and lots of swashbuckling. Luke loved it.

People had made a huge effort with the costumes, and there were probably a hundred Jack Sparrow looka-likes; some were so convincing, Johnny Depp himself could have turned up dressed as his alter ego and no one would have batted an eye. There were some, like Luke, who had gone all out with rings, belts, pouches, swords and hats, and some who were simply wearing t-shirts with skulls and crossbones on them. But there was only one octopus. He watched Flick run across the village green like the Pied Piper, waving her tentacles in the air as she was chased by a crowd of children all screeching and laughing at her. She had the biggest smile on her face, mirrored by the one he had on his own.

'You're in love with her, aren't you?' Quinn asked as he moved to Luke's side.

Luke nodded. 'Yeah I am.'

Quinn clapped him on the back. 'I'm happy for you, she seems lovely. I'm sorry your escape to Scotland didn't work out, I know you were excited about that, but selfishly I'm glad you'll be staying. I'd have missed you.'

'I'm not sure if I'm staying,' Luke said.

'What? But you love her, why would you walk away from that?'

'I have no idea if she feels the same.'

'She adores you, anyone can see that.'

'I know she likes me, and we're having a lot of fun together but I don't know if she sees a future with us.'

'You need to talk to her.'

'Of course I do and I will. But I have a few weeks before I go and I'm having way too much fun with her right now to want to screw it up by telling her I love her. That's how my last two relationships came to a crashing end. I'll tell her before I leave. That way if she doesn't feel the same I don't have to see her every day and feel my heart breaking.'

Luke stared at the beer in his hand that was clearly making him spill all his secrets today – and it was only his first one.

'What if she's holding herself back because you're leaving and seemingly giving her no indication you intend to stay?' Quinn said. 'Maybe telling her now would allow her to go all in and let herself fall in love with you too.'

He frowned; that did make a lot of sense.

'Look, you don't necessarily have to tell her you love her now, but just talk to her and tell her this is something serious for you. If she feels the same you can stay to see if it's something more, something worth fighting for.'

Luke knew Quinn was right. He could at least offer to stay a bit longer; the house in Scotland wasn't going anywhere and it would always be there if things ended, even if that was a few months from now. At least then he could say he'd given it his best shot. There was no rush to leave just because he was getting the keys on Monday and he needed to tell Flick that.

'Since when did you become so wise with regards to relationships? How's your love life?'

He watched Quinn's eyes move to where Alex was playing with her daughter. 'Ah, dishing out advice and taking it are two very different things. One is definitely much harder than the other.'

'Yeah, I hear you,' Luke sighed, taking another swig of his beer. But somehow he was going to have to find the courage to tell Flick what was in his heart or risk losing her for good.

CHAPTER FIFTEEN

Flick woke as the sun kissed her face. She opened her eyes watching the sun peep over the sea. It was going to be another glorious day.

Today was the grand opening of the Wonky Tree Studios and Flick had worked hard putting posters and leaflets everywhere in town, doing Facebook posts, running Facebook and Instagram ads and generally trying to get the word out as much as she could.

Polly was going to be ready with enough tea and cake to feed a small army and all the artists were going to be demonstrating or working on their art as people walked around.

The best part, or rather the scariest part, was that the local TV news was going to come and do a piece about how they had saved the tree and include the grand opening of the studios at the same time. It was going to be fabulous for publicity even though Flick was dreading having to stand in front of the camera and be interviewed by the journalists.

As if sensing her unease, Luke stroked her hair and she looked up at him as she lay on top of his chest. He smiled at her sleepily, clearly having just woken up.

She kissed his chest, right above his heart.

'Stop worrying. Everything is going to be great because you've worked your arse off to make sure this grand reopening will go without a hitch. All the artists have cheaper things displayed beautifully in their studios, the tree looks amazing, better than it ever did, and your interview with the journalists will go smoothly because you're passionate about saving the studios and the tree and you'll speak from the heart.'

She smiled. God she had fallen so hard for this man, she had never loved someone as much as she loved him. But he was due to complete on his house in Scotland the next day and a few weeks after that, as soon as all the work on the house was done, he'd be gone. He'd been on the phone with solicitors, estate agents, builders, decorators and landscapers and she could see how excited he was about it all.

There had been no conversation at all about what would happen between them once he left, whether they would continue a long-distance relationship or just say goodbye and wish each other well. In reality, how could a long-distance relationship work? Yes, she could fly to Edinburgh from Newquay or Exeter and then hire a car and drive the five hours from Edinburgh to Skye but wasn't the whole point of a long-distance relationship that ultimately they would be together, either in Scotland or here?

Luke wouldn't move back down here when he was so desperate to get away from the people of Lovegrove Bay and feasibly she couldn't leave when she had worked so hard to get the studios to be successful. Although she had no idea if it would be profitable enough for her nan to want to keep the place. She supposed if her nan decided to sell the place in six months anyway, she could move to Scotland then, if he wanted her. There wouldn't be anything left for her in Lovegrove Bay if her home, gift shop and the studios were taken away.

But what if Luke didn't want her there? What if Scotland was a fresh start for him and she wasn't part of it? She was desperate to talk to him about it, but she couldn't bring herself to start that conversation for fear of the answer. The fact that he hadn't raised it didn't fill her with joy. And she still couldn't forget how he reacted when she'd inadvertently told him she loved him. Admittedly, that was only the second time they'd made love and it was probably way too early to utter those words but was a week later any better? Had they really been together long enough to start planning a life together, long-distance or otherwise?

She had loved being with him since they got together, going for walks with him, chatting and cuddling with him. He made her laugh. And the sex was utterly incredible, every single time. She wasn't ready to say goodbye to all that yet. Or to him.

He stroked her face. 'Why are you looking so sad?'

She smiled and kissed his hand. 'Why are you so lovely?'

But he wasn't to be deterred. 'If there's something bothering you, you can talk to me.'

Here was the opening she so desperately wanted and she was too afraid to take it. If she told him she loved him and he didn't feel the same way she'd be heartbroken. She also didn't want to stand in the way of his exciting new life in Scotland. But she couldn't let him walk away without at least trying to save what they had.

She looked at her watch. If she was going to have that conversation, it wasn't going to be now. There was too much to get ready for the grand reopening.

She leaned up and kissed him. 'Everything is fine.'

Before he could say anything else, she quickly climbed out of bed and headed for the shower.

∼

Flick couldn't be happier right now. All of their hard work had well and truly paid off. The house looked great: fresh paint, newly arranged studios, polished floors, even the garden had been tidied with new plants and flowers to make it look welcoming. The tree, despite its sad demise, looked spectacular, lots of people had commented on it. Everyone loved the café and how beautifully it had been decorated in the bumblebee theme.

Hundreds of people had come through the doors

throughout the day, looking around at all the art, watching the artists at work, admiring the new café while they enjoyed their tea and cake. And Flick knew all the artists had made a good number of sales too, she just hoped that level of interest and trade would continue. The grand opening had been running all day, so people had come and gone rather than there being a deluge of visitors all at once and that had worked really well.

She'd had so many people come into her gift shop and had spent a long time talking to some of the customers about the different kits and craft paraphernalia she was selling. Being able to pass on that love of making art had filled her with so much joy. Some people had even bought her wish jars too, which made her happy.

The local news journalists had been there for a few hours, filming the tree, the artists' studios, the house, interviewing the artists, Polly and the visitors. It was going to be great publicity once it aired on the TV later that day.

All that was left was for them to interview her. They were setting up the camera and the microphone ready for her and she was frantically trying to remember her speech when Luke came over and took her hand.

'You're going to be great,' Luke said, kissing her head. 'It's your passion and belief in the studios that have led us to here. Just speak from the heart.'

She smiled. She loved his faith in her.

'Are you ready?' Sally, the reporter, asked.

Flick nodded and Luke took a step back out of shot, giving her two thumbs up for luck.

'Whenever you're ready just tell us about the studios, the tree and what it means to you and the people of the town,' Sally said, giving her an encouraging smile. 'And it doesn't need to be perfect, we'll edit it together over footage of the house and the tree, so don't worry about any mistakes, they'll be edited out.'

Flick nodded.

She looked at the camera and saw the little red light come on and Sally gave her a nod. She took a deep breath.

'My grandad opened the art studios here thirty years ago to showcase artists' work but mainly to support those with brain injuries by allowing them to express themselves through the medium of art. Therapeutic art is an important part of recovery and bringing that back to our community was something myself and the artists here are passionate about. Our wonky tree is synonymous with perseverance and resilience, which are things that people with brain injuries know about only too well, and so it was only right that we restored it back in its place just in time for the grand reopening today. We have something for everyone here, even if you just want to come up here for a coffee or a slice of Polly's delicious cake. There's beautiful artwork for you to buy and part of the money spent on every sale and every cup of tea will go towards running the art workshops here so it's a win for everybody. We're open seven days a week so please come down and have a look.'

Sally nodded and turned the camera off. 'That was perfect. You have a great place here and it's wonderful to see the community rallying behind it.'

Flick thought that the visitors were perhaps more concerned with the tree than the studios but their support here today was a good start.

She said goodbye to Sally and walked over to Luke who enveloped her in his arms.

'Good job,' he said, kissing the top of her head.

She smiled against his chest. She just had to hope it was enough.

CHAPTER SIXTEEN

Flick had just had a shower and was getting dressed in her room the next day when the phone rang. She saw the Australian country code and quickly answered it, sitting down on the bed to talk to her nan.

'Hello lovely, how's it all going there?' her nan asked.

'Brilliantly. We had our grand reopening, which was a huge success, we were even featured on the local news.'

'I saw it online. It looked fabulous and the café looks amazing. You've really done something incredible there.'

'We had a steady stream of visitors all day and a few days ago we held our first workshop for those with acquired brain injuries. We only had one person, Frank, who lost the ability to talk and walk in an accident last year. He and Luke made birdboxes and he loved it. I can't tell you how happy I am, everything is going wonderfully.'

'I knew you'd do something brilliant with it... However, I... umm, have some bad news.'

Her heart leapt. Nothing good could come from hearing those words.

'What's the news?' Flick said.

'I've decided to stay out here in Australia and to do that, and apply for permanent residency, I have to have some money in the account, a lot of money in fact. So I'm going to sell the house, I'm afraid.'

Flick's heart dropped into her stomach. 'Nan, no.'

'I know, I'm sorry, I really am. But that house has been like a millstone round my neck for several years now and I've come to resent it. I tried to keep it going, for Tom's sake – he loved the studios and what they meant to the community and I wanted to honour that for him. For fifteen years I tried my best and failed miserably to do that. For fifteen years I lived my life for a man who's dead rather than living my life for me. I always wanted to live in London or travel the world but I stayed because of your grandfather's legacy. And now, I've fallen in love again. Maxwell has been like a breath of fresh air and I feel like a young woman when I'm with him. And he told me he loves me too. And maybe it's too soon to change my whole life for a man I've only met a few weeks ago and maybe it's silly, impetuous and hasty but at my time of life I can't hang around for years before I make a decision. I need to grab life with both hands. And even if things don't work out with Maxwell, I've fallen in love with Australia too. I can buy a camper van and travel all the way round the coast, or I can use the money to travel, to see New Zealand, Thailand, Japan. But one thing is for sure, I don't want to come back to that house. I'm really sorry.'

Flick wanted to cry. 'But all our hard work, starting the café, the workshops… I've got new artists who have moved in, Luke's spent a fortune on Polly's utensils and new machines for the café and we spent ages creating the gift shop. All that was for nothing.'

'I know, but I can't keep that house for you either, I'm sorry. And it hasn't been for nothing. As agreed, I'll give you six months before I put the house up for sale. If you can build it up to a successful, thriving business, maybe I can sell it to someone who will take on the business as it is, who will be happy to leave the artists in situ and run the workshops.'

Flick didn't think that was likely, letting the artists continue to stay there rent free was not an attractive selling point.

'I need to go,' Flick said.

'I really am sorry,' her nan said.

'I am too.'

She said her goodbyes and hung up, staring at the phone in shock.

There was a knock on the bedroom door and she looked up to see Luke looking at her with concern. 'You OK?'

She shook her head and tears spilled over her cheeks.

He quickly moved into the room and sat down on the bed next to her, wrapping her in his arms. 'What's wrong?'

'My nan is selling the house.'

'No, wait. She can't do that, she gave you six months to make it a success and you've already done so much in such a short amount of time, it's doing so well.'

'I know, but she says she doesn't want it anymore and was only keeping it going for my grandad and now she wants to live her life for her. She's fallen in love and says she isn't coming home.'

'Oh crap.'

'She says she'll still give us the six months to make a go of it and will try to sell it as a successful business. But who in their right minds would take this place on with the current terms? We're making some money but it's twenty-five percent of twenty or thirty pounds here and there. It's hardly going to set the world on fire.'

'But the workshops are important, I saw that with Frank, what a difference they can make to people. I saw it in my mum when she came home from attending them, they really help.'

'I know, I think that's the part I'm most sad about, that's the legacy I wanted to save. And the money from the café, the gift shop and the artists' work meant that we could offer those workshops for free. The new owner isn't going to continue doing that.' She wiped a tear away. 'Frank lit up after months of hell and I can't face taking that away from him again. And think of all the other people we could help in the same way. I don't want to walk away from that.'

'No, I don't either.'

'And selfishly, I don't know what this means for me. I

was loving my new life here, I love working in the gift shop so much, I love walking around the town and beaches, I love our clifftop walks as the sun sets.' She didn't tell Luke that it was him she loved spending time with the most on those walks. 'Once the studio is gone, I lose my home, my job, the whole reason I came down here in the first place. I guess I can try to get a little flat somewhere in the town, if I can find a job to fund it, but jobs in coastal towns are few and far between.'

'Let's not give up yet, I'm sure we can think of something,' Luke said. 'Let's round everyone up and have a meeting, maybe we can come up with a plan.'

He left the room and she quickly finished getting dressed although it was hard to find any hope. She wasn't sure what anyone could do to save the studios.

~

Flick walked into the café a short while later to find everyone there waiting for her – Luke had obviously rounded everyone up. She was so nervous about telling them. If she thought they'd been annoyed before, about changing the studios and making cheaper items, it was going to be so much worse now they'd all agreed to get behind it to save it. Everyone had worked so hard. How was Flick going to tell them that in a few months they would probably have to pack up and leave and that all their hard work had been for nothing? And while she understood her nan's reasons for selling, she was also annoyed that Audrey had left it to her to tell everyone the bad news. She really had washed her hands of it.

Flick sat down and cleared her throat. 'I just wanted to start by saying thank you all for your hard work over the last few days, creating smaller items, transforming your studio spaces and helping with the wonky tree. And thank you Polly, your hard work and delicious food has brought people through the doors. I think we've created something wonderful here and the importance of the workshops in helping those with brain injuries is something very close to my heart, and it seems, for many of you too.'

She swallowed the lump in her throat. 'I'm afraid there's no easy way to say this, but my nan has decided to sell regardless of what we've achieved.'

Predictably, there was an outcry, with everyone talking and shouting over each other, moaning about the work they'd put in, how it had all been a waste of time. She held her hands out to try to get them to be quiet and after a few moments they all stopped talking, obviously hoping for some chink of light in this dark cloud. Although Flick couldn't give them that. She explained her nan's reasons why and that she was still giving them six months and that her nan then hoped to sell the house as a successful business.

They were all quiet for a moment before they started speaking again.

'Well, that's rubbish,' Aidan said. 'Who would buy the studios as it is when they can make far more money by converting it into a hotel or B&B?'

'We've all worked so hard,' Ethel said.

'The café looks amazing,' Polly said. 'And I've just given up the lease on my van.'

'OK, OK,' Luke said. 'We're all upset by this and understandably so but this isn't Flick's fault. And I do understand why Audrey is doing this, this was Tom's dream, it was never hers. But rather than moan about it, we need to do something constructive and come up with a plan to save it.'

They were all quiet as they thought.

'I could ask everyone in the Wonky Tree Facebook group to donate to save it,' Ethel said.

'I think it's great that we raised enough money to resurrect the wonky tree, but that was thousands. We'd need over a million pounds to buy the house and I just can't see that we'd ever raise that kind of money,' Flick said.

'What about getting a local business to sponsor it?' Rose said. 'There's one in a nearby town, Pet Protagonist, who make personalised books for people's pets and donate a percentage of their profits to a local animal shelter. Maybe we can find a company who would be willing to help us in the same way?'

'But it's one thing a company giving us, say, a thousand pounds a month to go towards our workshops, but a company isn't just going to buy a million-pound house,' Flick said.

'What about asking a brain injury charity to buy it for us?' Aidan said. 'If they can see the importance of what we are doing here, they might help.'

'I don't think they will have the money for that, we all know charities are crying out for donations,' Flick said, feeling like she was shooting down every suggestion. And it wasn't like she could come up with something better.

They all fell quiet as their ideas dried up. Flick noticed that Polly was staring at Luke, clearly expecting him to swoop in and save the day like he had in the past. And this was why Luke wanted to leave Lovegrove Bay. Every time something went wrong or when something was broken, it was Luke who was expected to pay out and fix it. No one liked him for him, they liked him for what he could do for them and that had to be exhausting. Flick had no doubt if she was to ask him to buy the house, he would do it because he had a heart of gold, but that was exactly why she never would. She wouldn't take advantage of him like that.

'I think we have to be practical,' Flick said. 'I hate to say it when you've all worked so hard but the most important thing to save is the workshops, that's the legacy my grandad created when he started this place, that's what we've all rallied behind. We can make a real difference to people's lives. We can approach companies to sponsor something like that, hire the church hall once or twice a week with the sponsor money and continue to teach our art to people with brain injuries. We can get other art teachers to teach them too, a different workshop each week.'

'And what about the rest of us?' Rose said.

Flick sighed. 'I don't know. There was never any

guarantee any of this would work. I guess we just keep on doing what we're doing now, we keep running the studios and hope for some miracle over the next six months and, in the meantime, you should keep looking around for your own studio space. Polly, the café is a big success so far, that will look good for any potential buyers. Maybe someone will buy the place purely for a successful business like yours.'

They were all quiet, the joy and excitement of seeing life breathed back into this place over the last few days well and truly gone. Slowly they all got up and trudged out and Polly went back into the kitchen, leaving just Flick and Luke.

She moved to sit next to him, taking his hand. He was looking thoughtful.

'Promise me something,' Flick said.

'What?'

'That you're not going to go white knight in shining armour with this.'

'I can't promise that.'

'You don't have to fix everything, it's not your responsibility. Sometimes things just don't work out, that's life, that's the way it is. You can't save everybody.'

'But I have the money, and I can spend it how I see fit.'

'I will be really angry if you do this.'

He frowned. 'Why?'

'Because you're not a cash cow. Why should you bail us out, it isn't fair. As I told you before, throwing money at it isn't the answer.'

'But it is, it will solve all your problems.'

'No, Luke, I don't want your money. We'll be fine without it. As long as we can save the workshops in some capacity, I'll be happy.'

'But what will you do?'

She shrugged. 'I don't know, I'll be OK, I always am. I'll stay in Lovegrove Bay long enough to establish the weekly workshops for those with brain injuries in the church hall or some other venue. If I can find a job then I'll stay here, if not I'll move on somewhere else, go where the work is.'

'But this is your home.'

She resisted saying that without him, it wouldn't be, but she decided to be a little brave. 'I suppose I could always move to Scotland with you.'

She was only half joking, but she wondered what his reaction to it would be.

'No. This isn't right. We'll fix this. We'll find a way. You belong here, you have to stay here.'

He got up and walked out and she was left staring after him.

That felt like a very emphatic no to her going to Scotland with him and that left her feeling very confused about what kind of future they might have.

~

Flick was busily working in the gift shop later. There was a couple in there looking around at all the craft kits and whereas ordinarily that would make her so happy she couldn't find any joy in it today. It just seemed so pointless, building a business up to be a big success to lose it all in a few months.

She looked up as Luke ran upstairs to the mezzanine to talk to her.

'All sorted,' Luke said.

'What?'

'You don't have to worry about losing the studios.'

Her heart sank. 'Luke, you haven't, please tell me you haven't bought it.'

'It seemed the obvious solution.'

Her hands went to her face, making her look like *The Scream* by Edvard Munch. 'Luke, you can't buy me a million-pound house, that's insane.'

'I didn't buy it for you, it's not yours, it's in my name. Consider it an investment. I'll still get twenty-five percent of all profits for the rest of my life.'

'That's not how investments work. Investments like this are only worth it if you pay off the money you've spent after a few years. It doesn't matter how successful we are, we are never ever going to be able to pay back a million pounds. Why would you do that?'

'The workshops are too important. The difference we made to one person is more than worth it, but the help you can give to hundreds or thousands of people over the years is the best thing I could ever spend my money on. And I wanted to do it for you. You belong here. This house, this town, it's your home. The gift shop is your dream. And you're making a difference, I want you to continue doing that.'

'Luke, no, I can't let you do this.'

'It's my money to do with what I want. And I want to do this.'

'I can't accept it.'

'It's not yours to accept, I've bought a house, you're just going to be in charge of it.'

'What if I don't want it?'

'It's a done deal.'

'Well undo it, take it back, tell Audrey you've changed your mind.'

'No.'

Flick was trembling and tearful over the shock of what he'd done. She couldn't even feel any relief or joy right now, she felt kind of numb. And angry and frustrated that her fairy godfather had swooped in to save her one more time. She didn't want him to waste his money like this.

He smiled. 'Why are you being so difficult? Most people would say thank you and then celebrate.'

'I don't feel that you wasting a million pounds is anything to celebrate. I just can't get my head around you doing something like this. Most boyfriends might buy their girlfriends a bunch of flowers or a box of chocolates.'

'I wanted to make you happy.'

She stared at him, a huge lump forming in her throat. Then she moved over to him and took his face in her hands. 'Thank you, so much. You have no idea what this means.'

'I do and that's why I did it.'

She smiled and hugged him and he wrapped his arms around her. Her mind was a whirl of emotions. Relief and happiness were obviously at the forefront, she was delighted that her home, the studios and the workshops would be saved. She was in shock over Luke's generosity. But she couldn't ignore the niggle at the back of her head that he'd paid a million pounds to stop her from moving to Scotland with him.

'Oh I've got the keys to the house, the house in Scotland is now officially mine.'

Talk about rubbing salt in the wound. She forced a smile onto her face and looked up. 'Congratulations, I'm really happy for you.'

He studied her. 'You are?'

'Of course, it's a new start for both of us.'

She swallowed a lump in her throat. A new start that was hundreds of miles apart. She couldn't find anything to be happy about that.

CHAPTER SEVENTEEN

Flick let herself into her flat later that day feeling emotionally drained. From the disappointment of losing the house, the frustration and shock of Luke swooping into save them, the relief of saving the house and what that meant for their relationship, she'd been on an emotional rollercoaster.

Luke had told Polly and the other artists he intended to buy the place but would only keep it if it was self-sufficient. He'd made it clear that the twenty-five percent profits they gave him had to be enough to cover all the bills and overheads because he didn't want any of them resting on their laurels and slipping back into old ways. They'd all committed to keep doing what they were doing now as it was clearly working so well.

So that was it, the house was saved, so why did she feel so flat about that? It was everything she wanted. Except it wasn't. There was something she wanted far more than that, something money could never buy.

Her phone rang in her pocket and she fished it out to see it was Tabitha. Luke wasn't back yet but she wanted to talk to her friend in private so she shut herself in her bedroom.

'Hey lovely,' Flick said as she sat cross-legged on the bed.

'Hey gorgeous, how goes the world's greatest love story?'

Flick sighed and tears pricked her eyes. 'Unfortunately I don't think it's that.'

'Oh no, what happened? The last time we spoke you were telling me how you'd fallen head over heels in love with the man.'

She'd spoken to Tabitha a couple of times and Tabitha always wanted to know every detail of their relationship. Although she hadn't gone into detail about their sex life, much to Tabitha's disappointment, she had told her everything else, including how fast and hard she had fallen for him.

'I've been dreading having that conversation with him, about what happens when he leaves for Scotland in a few weeks in case he's decided that we've had a great time but that's it.'

'I don't think that's the case. From everything you've told me, the man is as smitten as you are.'

'Well today, my nan phones to tell me she's selling the house as she's fallen in love with someone in Australia.'

'Whoa, good for Audrey.'

'I know, I'm happy for her.'

'But that means you'll lose your home and the studios you so desperately wanted to save.'

'Yes exactly. I tell Luke and jokingly suggest that I could move with him to Scotland. The next thing he's bought the house from Audrey so I can stay here and we can continue doing the workshops.'

'Well that's great news...' The penny clearly dropped. 'You think he did that to stop you moving to Scotland with him.'

'No, I think he did it because he's incredibly kind and generous. But my life is here now for the foreseeable future and he must have known that when he agreed to buy the house. If we are to have any kind of long-distance relationship, surely that's with the end goal of being together at some point, either here or in Scotland or somewhere in between, but he's made sure that I can't really leave. And I wanted this, I wanted a life here, I want to save the workshops more than anything, and I have my gift shop which is a dream come true. But he's not going to come back here just for me when he wanted to get so far away from Lovegrove Bay that he bought a house in Scotland. So where does that leave us?'

'Ah yes, I see.'

'And now I'm thinking that he made this decision to buy the house so easily, there wasn't a thought for one second about what that means for us. So maybe our relationship isn't the greatest love story after all, maybe it was only ever a fling, just great sex, just a bit of fun. And I'm trying really hard to get my head round that.'

'It is a very generous gift, the kind of thing you do for someone you love,' Tabitha said. 'Knowing how much the house meant to you, maybe he sacrificed your relationship to make you happy.'

'Oh god Tabby, *he* makes me happy, I love him. There has to be a way to make this work.'

'Honestly, I think you have to talk to him about all of this. I'm sure you can figure it out if you just talk.'

Flick sighed. She knew Tabby was right but she only hoped it wasn't too late for that.

~

Luke let himself into the flat and, noticing that Flick's bedroom door was closed, he walked over to ask her if she wanted to go out for dinner. He wanted to talk to her about their future, about him staying in Lovegrove Bay a bit longer to see if they had something worth fighting for. He raised his hand to knock and realised she was on the phone. He was just about to turn away when he heard some of what she was saying.

'… it was only ever a fling, just great sex, just a bit of fun.'

His heart fell into his stomach as he moved quickly away from the door. He'd been wanting to talk to Flick about their future but that was his answer: they didn't have one. And he'd never felt so utterly heartbroken before.

~

Flick was sitting next to Luke on the roof later that night. He'd been very quiet all evening and she didn't know why.

She took his hand and leaned into his shoulder.

'I'm going to go up to my new house tomorrow,' Luke said.

She sat up to look at him in shock. 'I thought you'd be here until the renovations are finished.'

He shook his head. 'There are complications with it. I need to go up there to oversee everything.'

'How long will you be gone?'

'I'll be there until it's all finished, then I'll pop back for a few days to collect my things and that's it, I'll be gone.'

'Oh god Luke, I thought I had more time with you.' Tears pricked her eyes. 'I'm going to miss you so much.'

He frowned as he stared at her. 'I'll miss you too.'

'I've loved spending time with you since I've come here.'

He swallowed. 'I've loved it too.'

Her heart was hammering against her chest as she plucked up courage for what she wanted to say next. 'I could… come up and see you.'

He frowned. 'I don't think that's a viable option.'

Her heart crashed into her stomach in disappointment.

'A fourteen-hour drive is no fun and if you fly it's still going to take the whole day with arriving at the airport two hours before departure, a two-hour flight and then a further five-hour drive once you reach the other end. You do that journey a few times, pretty soon you'd start resenting it.'

'I wouldn't resent seeing you.'

His eyes softened and he stroked her face, then he let his hand drop.

'And you'd be making the journey the opposite way too. If you wanted to see me, that is. Would you resent that?' she asked.

He shook his head. 'No, but I just don't think it would work. How often would we see each other, once a week, once a month? You travel up there, spend one day with me and travel back, that's three days you're not here in the studio. How often could you feasibly do that and successfully run the studios and oversee the workshops?'

She supposed he made a good point but she couldn't bear thinking of the alternative and never seeing him again.

'So you don't even want to try?'

He frowned. 'We can try but I think all that travelling back and forth would start wearing thin for you, pretty soon you'd be making excuses not to come and your visits would get less and less.'

'It sounds like you've given up already.'

'Flick, I have loved the last week so much, we've had a lot of fun and the sex has been incredible but you're not going to keep travelling up and down the UK just for great sex.'

Oh, that hurt so much. She let go of his hand. 'No, I suppose not.'

They fell into silence which for the first time was horrendously awkward. This was it, this was the end.

'I have to be up really early tomorrow morning to get my flight so it's probably best you sleep in your own bed tonight,' Luke said.

'Right, yes, of course,' Flick said, her voice quiet.

He gave her a kiss on the cheek. 'I'll see you in a few weeks.'

With that he got up and went down the stairs, leaving her alone on the roof. The tears she had been holding back fell down her cheeks.

~

Flick was woken by soft noises from the lounge a few hours later. She looked at the clock and saw it was just coming up to three in the morning. Clearly Luke was on his way out. She scrambled out of bed before her brain could talk herself out of it. She opened the door and saw he was walking towards the front door with a bag in his hand.

He stared at her in surprise and she ran forward, wrapped her arms around him and kissed him hard. He immediately dropped the bag and gathered her in his arms as he kissed her back. The tears she thought were gone came flooding back.

He pulled back to look at her and frowned when he saw her crying. 'Why are you crying?'

'Because I'm going to miss you so much.'

His frown deepened and when he spoke his voice was rough. 'I'm going to miss you too.'

'Will you text me when you get there so I know you're safe?'

He nodded and looked at his watch. 'I really have to go.'

She reached up and kissed him again, stroking his face. She pulled back to look at him. 'Getting over you is going to be the hardest thing I've ever done.'

His eyes widened. Then he gave her another brief kiss on the head and walked out the door.

CHAPTER EIGHTEEN

Flick had cried so many times that morning and it wasn't even nine o'clock. Every time she thought she had stopped, she'd find herself thinking about him and the tears would start all over again.

It all seemed so final, so quick. One minute she had been head over heels in love with Luke and the way he had been looking at her she felt sure he felt the same. The next moment he was buying her the house which had put paid to any tentative thoughts she might have had about moving to Scotland with him, telling her it was just great sex and then leaving. Yes, he'd be back in a few weeks, but only for a few days to pack up all his stuff then he'd be gone for good.

Had it really all been one-sided? Had she seen what she wanted to see? Somehow, she didn't believe that. Tabitha was right, buying the house for her was an incredibly generous gift, Luke obviously cared for her a great deal to want to do that.

Maybe they should have had a conversation earlier about where this was going and if it had a future, then she wouldn't have been so disappointed when it came to an end. But dating for such a short time seemed too early for talks of the future. She thought she had more time.

Maybe she should have taken the bull by the horns and told him she loved him. Even if it had never led anywhere, at least he would have known he was loved. He deserved that. After his last relationship where Martine laughed at him then dumped him when he told her he loved her, and with Sophie telling him she only saw him as a friend, he thought he was unlovable when nothing could be further from the truth. Flick loved him, completely and utterly, and she should have given him that.

She sat up from where she was flopped on the sofa. She wanted him to have that. Even if it changed nothing, even if he didn't feel the same, she wanted him to know he was loved, even if it was nothing more than a goodbye gift.

She grabbed her phone to call him before remembering he'd probably be on the plane right then or at least driving the five hours from Edinburgh to Skye. Besides, something like that should really be done face to face.

Making a snap decision, she decided she would book a flight and go and see him. She certainly didn't want to wait a few weeks to have this conversation. She did a quick search for flights and, while there wasn't one from

Newquay that day or the next, there was one from Exeter that night, which would be a bit more of a drive but it was doable. She quickly booked it before she could talk herself out of it. After today there were no more workshops until next week, she could fly out tonight and fly back the next day. The gift shop would just have to close for a couple of days. This suddenly felt too important.

Having made the decision, she felt a little better. It probably wouldn't have the outcome she wanted, but at least he'd know.

She quickly had a shower, got dressed and went downstairs to help Rose with her painting workshop.

She bumped into Quinn as he was heading towards his own studio.

He frowned when he saw her. 'Hey, you OK? You look like you've been crying.'

The tears she thought had gone filled her eyes again. 'Luke left. We're basically finished. He's going up to oversee the renovations on his new house and then he said he would just be popping back to pack all his stuff and then leave for good.'

'Yeah, he told me.'

'Everything was so perfect between us, I'm not sure what went wrong.'

'Yeah, he was pretty smitten with you, I thought he'd end up staying here but then...' he trailed off.

'But then what?'

Quinn chewed his lip as he studied her. 'He heard you, on the phone last night, saying it was just great sex, just a bit of fun. He was heartbroken, he thought this was something more for the two of you.'

'Wait, what? I never said that.'

'That's what he heard.'

She frantically tried to remember her conversation with Tabby the night before and what Luke could have heard to make him think that.

She gasped. 'No, that's what I told my friend I thought he thought.'

'What?' Quinn said in confusion.

She sighed. 'As the house was going to be sold, I offered to come to Scotland with him and then he bought the house. I was chatting to my friend Tabby saying, well he clearly didn't want me to come to Scotland with him, and I said, maybe he thinks all this was just great sex, just a bit of fun. That's what he heard me say and thinks that's how I feel.'

'Christ, you two really need to talk to each other.'

'I know, I wanted to, but I thought we had more time. It didn't feel right bringing up a future so soon after we'd met. And last night I asked him about seeing him again, I said I would come up and see him in Scotland and he said there was no point going all that way just for great sex. God, that's why he said that.'

Her heart broke that she'd hurt him in that way.

'Call him, explain that he was wrong,' Quinn said. 'I bet he'd be on the next plane home. He… adores you.'

She shook her head. 'I've booked a flight, I'm going to see him tonight. I thought if it was going to end, he should at least know that I love him. I wanted to tell him to his face. I didn't know if it would change anything but I wanted him to know.'

A huge smile grew on Quinn's face. 'You love him?'

'Yes, so much.'

'And you're flying to Scotland to tell him that?'

'Yes.'

'A big gesture, he's going to love that.'

An idea suddenly formed in her mind. 'Yes, a big romantic gesture.'

She smiled as she came up with her plan and suddenly tonight couldn't come soon enough.

~

After making a quick phone call, she hurried into Rose's studio ready to help with her painting workshop. They had three people coming today, Chloe, Amy and Michael. The three of them were friends after meeting each other at other local brain injury support groups a few years before. While their recovery and rehabilitation meant they were able to continue living the lives they had before their injury, to a large extent, the impact of their injuries had left them with other problems.

Because their issues were mental rather than physical, Rose didn't need any help today, but she wanted Flick there as moral support. Flick joined her in her studio a few minutes before the guests arrived.

'So what do you have planned for today?' Flick said, taking a seat at the large table Rose had set up in the middle of the room so they could all work together.

'We're doing finger painting,' Rose said, a big smile on her face.

Flick cringed. The last thing she wanted to do was patronise them, especially not with something so childish. 'Isn't that a bit simplistic?'

'I tried it last night and as someone who has been painting professionally for nearly twenty years, let me tell you, I loved it. It was so freeing, and the feel of handling the paint with my fingers was wonderful. It also puts us all on a bit more of an even keel. My expertise as a painter largely comes from the skill of handling a brush. Without that I'm pretty much useless. I think it will be a good way to help express their emotions about how their injury has affected them.'

Flick still wasn't so sure and that must have shown on her face.

'Why don't you try it today for yourself before you're so quick to judge? Also I'll give them the option, they can use brushes if they prefer.'

'I think that's a good idea and yes, I'm happy to join in with whatever you have planned. Right, I'll go and meet them.'

She stood back up and walked down the hall towards the front door, trying not to look at Luke's empty studio in case she started crying all over again.

She opened the door just as three people and a dog were walking up towards it.

'Hello, are you here for the workshop?'

'Yes hello, I'm Amy, this is Chloe, Michael and this

handsome chap is Charlie,' Amy said, referring to the black labrador.

Flick knew Charlie was Michael's emotional support dog and went everywhere with him.

'Hi, I'm Flick, I'm sort of in charge here. You'll be working with Rose today doing some painting.'

They all said hello.

'Is it OK to stroke Charlie? I don't want to disturb him if he's working,' Flick said.

'Oh no, you can stroke him,' Michael said. 'He'd be most offended if you didn't.'

Flick laughed and gave Charlie some ear scratches. His head was velvety soft and stroking him made a little of the pain she was feeling ebb away. Maybe she needed to get herself a dog. He could join her on her morning and evening walks around the town and clifftops and it would be nice to have someone to talk to so she didn't feel so alone. She pushed thoughts about Luke away.

'I'll take you down to Rose's studio,' Flick said.

She walked back down the hall and they followed her. Rose was waiting nervously and smiled when she saw them.

'Hello, come in, I'm Rose.'

Flick did the introductions, making sure to include Charlie who seemed to be constantly wagging his tail.

They all sat down and Flick took coffee and tea orders and then phoned them up to Polly who was going to come down shortly with cakes, biscuits and Danishes.

'So before we start, I wonder if you might feel

comfortable talking about what you struggle with just so we can have a better understanding of what you're going through,' Rose said, gently. 'No worries if you'd prefer not to.'

'I don't mind,' Amy said. 'I think what I struggle with most is people's attitudes towards me. Friends, well not close friends but acquaintances or colleagues will say things like, "Oh but you look so normal," like they expect someone with a brain injury to be fully incapacitated, unable to walk, talk, feed or dress themselves. And of course there are those who have suffered horrendously with their injuries, much more so than me, so I'm very lucky in that regard. But a visible injury or disability is so much easier to understand and empathise with. No one can see my disability so they just expect me to carry on like I was before I had my stroke. They'll say things like, "Are you back to normal now?" which is just offensive, like my struggles make me abnormal.'

She shook her head and took a sip of water. 'In reality, this, what I'm dealing with now, will probably always be my new normal. And eighty percent of the time, I'm fine, I don't feel any different to how I was before my stroke. But when I'm tired I speak a lot slower, I find it difficult to form the words and I have to concentrate really hard on getting each word out. That makes me feel very self-conscious and not want to talk at all, unless I'm with these guys who understand or very close friends or family. At work, I really struggle towards the end of the day and my colleagues just don't get it. They see me chatting away normally like I am now at the start of the day and by the end I'm stumbling over my words, stuttering, and I know some of them think I'm putting it on. And that's what's so great about workshops like this and making friends like these two – they get it like no one else does.'

Flick smiled at that. The workshops weren't just about giving participants an artistic or creative outlet, they were about making friends or talking to others who were in the same boat and that's why they were so important.

Chloe nodded. 'I'm the same as Amy in many ways but I will often substitute one word for another completely unrelated word. Ordering a cheese sandwich, for example, would likely turn into a request for a coathanger sandwich. It's just one word in a completely normal sentence but it obviously stands out like a sore thumb. Everyone finds it really funny when I do it and that used to upset me. Now I can laugh at how ridiculous it is too but sometimes I find it really frustrating because the right word just won't come. Again, it mostly happens when I'm tired, but sometimes I can surprise myself. Sometimes I don't even know I've done it until people start looking at me strangely and I have to figure out which word I've said wrong. But like Amy it's people's expectations that are the hardest to deal with. They see me hiking up mountains or running marathons and don't expect me to have trouble doing something as simple as talking.'

'You two have hit the nail on the head,' Michael said. 'I can do everything I could do before my motorbike accident. I walked away with barely a scratch on me so everyone assumes I'm fine. I don't even have language difficulties like these two lovely ladies. Everything on the surface is perfect. But I get so emotional and tearful over the slightest thing, which apparently is very common for people with brain injuries. I get told to man up, or that real men don't cry, and I'm ashamed to admit, before the accident, that I thought it was weak to cry as a man. Now I can't seem to stop. It is getting better, it might only be two or three times a week that I cry now rather than every day, but it's the tiniest thing that will set me off. I can't even say I'm depressed, not really. Most days I'm absolutely fine but then I'll go to grab a banana from the fruit bowl and realise I ate the last one the day before and the tears will start. It's the most ridiculous thing. But people's attitudes to a grown man crying are just shocking, I've literally lost friends over it. Charlie here is a real help. When he sees I'm upset he will cuddle up to me or put his head on my lap and stroking him helps, it really does. And having Amy and Chloe to talk to. They get it.'

'I can understand having Charlie helps, I think we all need a Charlie in our lives,' Flick said.

'He's been a godsend,' Michael said, stroking Charlie's head.

'I think that's the thing about brain injuries, they affect everyone so differently,' Rose said. 'There is no one size fits all. Well, thank you for sharing your struggles. Talking about it really does help people to understand what you are going through. So today we are going to be painting with acrylics and, if you're willing to get your hands dirty, I thought we could all use our fingers instead of brushes. Although if you prefer, I have a load of different-sized brushes you can use instead. You can choose to paint whatever you want, perhaps something that represents your frustrations with your injury or, if you don't know what to paint, I thought we could all paint our famous wonky tree outside. You can paint realistically or use bright colours, you can paint in the style of Monet or Picasso, whatever you choose. There is no right or wrong today.'

'I love the idea of finger painting,' Amy said.

'I do too,' Chloe said.

Michael shrugged. 'I'm happy to give anything a try.'

Flick smiled as they got their paints ready and started using their hands and fingers to create their masterpieces, laughing and squealing at the feel of the paint. She felt an ache in her chest, wishing Luke was here to see this.

CHAPTER NINETEEN

Flick was definitely regretting her big romantic gesture right about now. She had been laughed at, had her photo taken and several people had made very unkind comments over the last few hours since she'd walked into Exeter airport and boarded her flight. She'd just got off in Edinburgh and was walking through the airport and still the pointing and laughing were continuing.

It was just after eight at night, she was tired and all she wanted to do was curl up and go to sleep. Stupidly she hadn't checked out the opening times of the car hire place. She'd assumed that she would get off the plane and pick up a car pretty much straightaway, but they were only open until six and didn't reopen now until eight the following morning.

She was going to have to get a hotel for the night and then make the five-hour journey to Skye tomorrow.

And she looked like an idiot. That was her biggest regret.

She walked outside into the cool night and looked around. Fortunately, there was a hotel dead opposite so she was having some luck today.

As she was still getting wolf whistled and mocked, she hurried across the road and walked into the reception area and stopped dead because Luke was walking out into the reception area too, dragging his suitcase behind him, having clearly come down from one of the bedrooms. She didn't understand what he was doing here, he should have been in Skye hours ago.

He was wearing his sexy glasses again and he looked tired. He obviously hadn't seen her yet, even though she stuck out like a sore thumb. She couldn't move, frozen to the spot, so she waited for him to see her. Suddenly he did and his eyes widened as he stopped dead in the middle of the lobby. He took in what she was wearing and his eyes widened even more, the bag he was holding dropping to the floor.

He approached her slowly as if he didn't believe she was really there and expected her to disappear any moment.

He reached out to touch her face but he didn't say anything.

'Luke, what are you doing here? I thought you'd be in your house in Skye by now?'

'I'm an idiot and as soon as the plane took off this morning I realised what an idiot I was. So I decided to fly back home and tell you personally.'

'You… you were going to fly home to tell me you're an idiot?' she asked, even more confused.

'Yes, I'm booked on the ten o'clock flight. What are you doing here?' His eyes cast down her body again. 'And why are you dressed as Arwen?'

Flick was so embarrassed that she'd chosen to come here dressed as the elf princess from *Lord of the Rings*, complete with pointy ears. It seemed like a good idea at the time when she'd come up with her plan that morning. When they'd watched the *Lord of the Rings* film the week before with the big scene where Arwen gives Aragorn her Evenstar necklace as a symbol of her love and commitment to give up her immortality for him, Luke had said that he didn't think any woman would ever love him enough to do that. So she'd decided to prove him wrong.

But now, standing before him dressed as an elf, she thought she'd made a big mistake. She didn't want him to think she wasn't taking their relationship seriously.

His eyes cast over her costume again. 'You look so beautiful,' he said, softly.

Emboldened by this, she took off the replica Evenstar necklace that came with the costume and pressed it into his hand. 'I came to give you this.'

He stared at it in his hand for the longest moment and she willed him to say something, anything to give her some hope that all was not lost.

Without a word, he took her hand and walked back over to the lifts, grabbing his bag on the way, her own bag dragging behind them. When the lift arrived he bundled her inside. The lift doors closed and he pressed the button for the top floor. But still he didn't say anything, he just kept on staring at the necklace in his hand.

She stroked his face and he tore his eyes away from the necklace to look at her. She saw he had tears in his eyes and she reached up to stroke them away.

'Luke, I'm sorry you heard what you did when I was on the phone, but you misunderstood. When you bought the house for me you did it without any thought about how it would affect our future. Buying Wonky Tree Studios meant I was tied to there and with you determined to leave I thought that you didn't see a future for us. So I was chatting to Tabitha about how maybe it was only sex for you, just a few weeks of fun and it was never meant to be anything more than that. That's what you heard.'

He shook his head and when he spoke his voice was rough. 'You belong there. You've started to build a life there and you've created something wonderful and important with the studios and the workshops. I couldn't let that be taken away from you. Buying the house was the only solution. And I didn't think about our future, as much as I wanted one with you, because you loving me just didn't appear on my radar. Especially after you said you loved me as a friend. I've been down that road before – women love me as a friend, they don't fall in love with me and want forever with me. It was only when you said that getting over me was the hardest thing you'd ever have to do and were crying over me leaving that I realised we might have something worth fighting for. Unfortunately, in my sleepy, emotional state, I didn't realise that until I was already on the plane flying away from there and then I had to wait for the next plane home. But you have to understand that I didn't buy you the house to get rid of you, I bought it because I wanted to make you happy and because Lovegrove Bay is your home.'

'But it's not, not without you. You make me happy, Luke Donnelly, and I would give up the studios, my home, the gift shop, I'd give it all up to be with you, wherever you are in the world. You are my home. I love you. I fell for you so fast and so hard and I've never felt this way before about anyone.'

He stared at her and then kissed her hard.

The lift doors pinged open and Luke quickly marched down the hall, almost dragging her and her bag behind him. He fished his key card out of his pocket, opened the room and walked in, pulling her with him. Before the door had even closed behind them, he was kissing her again. She wrapped her arms around him, pressing herself up against him and kissing him back. Her heart soared, this was where she belonged. And maybe he didn't love her yet, it was still so early for them, but this gave her so much hope, when that morning she'd had none.

She started wrestling him out of his t-shirt which was quite hard when their bodies were pressed together but she somehow managed it. He was already struggling to get her out of the dress.

'Careful, I have to return this,' Flick said.

'Oh hell no, we're keeping this dress. In fact, I might have to make love to you while you wear it.'

'The pointy ears do it for you? Do they turn you on?'

'You turn me on, regardless of what you wear. In fact the moment I realised I was head over heels in love with you was when you were dressed as an octopus.'

She laughed and then stopped. 'You… love me?'

'I love you, with everything I have.' Tears pooled in her eyes and he stroked them away. 'I love you so much.'

She reached up and kissed him again and he quickly removed her dress. He laid her down on the bed and paused just long enough to take off his jeans and she wrestled herself out of her knickers so she was naked before he was climbing back up over her and kissing her again, his hands caressing all over her. His hand slid up her thigh and touched her where she needed him the most. She moaned in relief, against his lips. He took her higher and higher, working his wonderful magic with his fingers until she was crying out against his lips.

He pulled back and leaned over the bed to grab a condom from his jeans. A few moments later he was inside her, staring down at her with complete adoration.

She stroked his face. 'Tell me again.'

'I love you.'

Her heart soared with happiness. 'I love you too.'

'Enough to give up your immortality to be with me?'

She grinned, stroking his face. 'Yes, the big, epic, fill-your-heart-to-the-top, last-forever kind of love.'

He smiled and kissed her and then moved his mouth so

he kissed right over her heart and it was that sweetest gesture, knowing she was loved, that made her fall apart around him. Then she was flying, soaring high, shouting out his name, telling him she loved him as he fell apart too.

They stared at each other breathless. She only realised she was crying again as he gently kissed her tears away.

After a few moments she found the energy to talk.

'So does this mean you'll be open to a long-distance relationship now? We can work it out. You can spend a weekend down there, I can spend the next weekend up here with you.'

'Oh god, absolutely not.'

'What?'

'I'm coming home with you, to stay.'

Her heart soared. 'But I don't want you to stay just for me.'

'But I do, because I love you and wherever you are, that's home for me.'

She smiled with love for him. 'But what about your house?'

'I can run it as a holiday let, an artists' retreat. Maybe get some of the local artists up here to run workshops with any potential artists who want to go. Maybe in a few years, once Wonky Tree Studios are up and running properly, we can spend a few months a year up here running workshops for those with acquired brain injuries.'

She smiled. 'I'd like that.'

'Yeah, I would too.'

'And I like that you're planning for our future.'

'Oh by then we'll be married, maybe with a baby on the way.'

Excitement bubbled through her and she scrambled up his chest to kiss him. 'I'd *really* like that.'

'Yeah, I would too.'

EPILOGUE

Flick looked out on the horizon as the boat, – or was it a yacht? – manoeuvred out of the pretty little harbour and made its way out to sea. The sun was just starting to set leaving trails of ruby and gold across the sky. It was beautiful.

Luke had hired the small yacht to celebrate her birthday, there was a pilot to take care of driving it and a chef who was going to cook them a meal. It was definitely above and beyond what she had been expecting.

'This is wonderful, you really didn't have to do this.'

'Oh I did, it's your birthday,' Luke said, sitting next to her and putting an arm around her shoulders. He kissed her forehead. 'Hiring this beautiful boat for the evening to spoil my incredible girlfriend on her birthday is money well spent.'

'You know I'd have been just as happy sitting on the beach eating a bag of chips. You didn't need to spend your money on this.'

'You never let me buy you anything. I had to do this in secret so you wouldn't stop me.'

'You bought me a house last year, just to make me happy. I think that was more than enough.'

'I bought the Wonky Tree Studios to help those with acquired brain injuries, not for you,' Luke said.

'You bought me a gift shop.'

'That was to support the studios, it wasn't really for you.'

'You bought me a peacock blue sofa with green and gold peacock feather cushions.'

'Our flat needed a new sofa, the old was getting a bit tatty.'

She smiled and leaned into him. He really was the kindest, most generous person she'd ever met. He'd also secretly donated half a million pounds to a local brain injury charity, ringfenced for art therapy or therapeutic art classes. He hadn't told her, but she'd seen the thank you letter in the flat and it had made her fall in love with him a little bit more, if that was at all possible.

It had been ten months since the Wonky Tree Studios had officially become Luke's, way ahead of the six months her nan had given them. Luke had said there was no point waiting until then to buy it when him taking it over gave peace of mind to the artists, but she'd known that was partly for her too.

Flick had wondered if he would be spending money like it was going out of fashion trying to keep it afloat, but the success of the café alone and twenty-five percent of its profits had given Luke enough money each month to pay all the bills and the overheads. So he was actually making a small profit each month when he got the money from the artists' sales too. He was putting all of that into a savings account to be used to pay for any repairs. While the money he got from the artists wasn't much, the studios were largely self-sufficient thanks to Polly and the artists' hard work in producing smaller items. But they'd all had the occasional large sale too, thanks to the extra footfall from the café, so everyone was happy. They'd all happily led the workshops too, including Aidan. Although the most popular workshop had been making Quinn's cutlery monsters, everyone had loved taking them home. There was at least one workshop a week now, and sometimes there were more.

They'd had more artists join them too as their reputation grew, everyone wanting to be a part of it. Every studio space was now taken up with various artists, it felt like a thriving little community again, just like it used to be, and Flick loved that.

Flick and Luke still lived in the little flat above the house because it just made sense when they both worked there. But Luke had converted the spare room into a little craft area for Flick to do her wish jars and other craft activities.

Flick looked up at Luke and couldn't help smiling. The last year had been incredible. The year before she had celebrated her birthday alone just a few days before she'd moved down here with no idea what she was going to do with her life, no job, no home, no prospects. Lovegrove

Bay was going to be a six-month stopgap but now she had a home in a beautiful seaside town, a job she loved, she'd saved her grandad's legacy and, to top it all, she'd found her soul mate, who she loved with all her heart.

'Look, dolphins,' Luke pointed and she stood up to see what he was looking at. Sure enough a pod of dolphins was keeping pace alongside the boat, leaping out of the water as they darted through the waves. They looked spectacular with the sun glinting off their wet, sleek bodies.

Suddenly the pod veered off and after a few moments she lost them from sight.

Flick looked back at Lovegrove Bay as they left it behind. all the different-coloured houses, the golden sandy beaches. This was home.

She looked at Luke. 'Are you happy here?'

He smiled. 'I'm the happiest I've ever been in my entire life.'

She leaned up and kissed him, smiling against his lips.

'Now I'm surprised you haven't utilised all the boat's facilities yet,' Luke said.

'What do you mean? Does it have a bed?' she ran a finger down the collar of his shirt, touching his warm chest.

'It absolutely does have a bed if you want a nap or… something later.'

'Something? Do you mean rumpy pumpy or mutually agreed nakedness?'

He smirked. 'Something like that. But I wasn't talking about the bed.'

Luke nodded towards the bow of the boat, which had the railings around the front, just like in the famous *Titanic* scene.

She let out a little gasp. 'Can I?'

'I've already cleared it with the skipper.'

She quickly scrambled up to the front and stuck her arms out so she was flying over the water. It was so much more exhilarating as they sped across the water. She felt Luke step up behind her and stick his arms out too as they flew together, their fingers touching just like in the film, just like they'd done the first night they met.

He wrapped his arms around her and held her close as she flew and she laughed at how closely he was replicating the film.

Then she felt him step back away from her and she turned around laughing only to find he was down on one knee behind her.

'Oh,' she said, her hands going to her face.

He reached out for her hand and she gave it to him.

'My beautiful Flick, I think I fell in love with you that first night you arrived in Lovegrove Bay, when we flew together on the rooftop, only I didn't realise it then. But my love for you has grown over the last year so that it's a part of me, something I carry with me everywhere I go. You have made me the happiest man alive and I will try, for the rest of my life, to make you as happy. Will you marry me?'

'Yes, of course I will, I love you so much. You have

turned my life upside down in the best possible way and I cannot imagine my life without you.'

He opened up the ring box and she saw a beautiful sapphire with a small diamond on either side. He slid it onto her finger and it fitted perfectly. He stood up and kissed her and she melted into him. He fitted her perfectly too.

She pulled back. 'I've just realised, if I marry you, I really will have to give up my immortality.'

He shook his head. 'No, you won't. The kind of love we have will last forever.'

If you enjoyed *The House on Waterfall Hill,* you'll love my next gorgeously romantic story, *The Cottage on Christmas Gardens*

A LETTER FROM HOLLY

Thank you so much for reading *The House on Waterfall Hill,* I had so much fun writing this story, creating the wonderful town of Lovegrove Bay and falling in love with the characters. I hope you enjoyed reading it as much as I enjoyed writing it.

One of the best parts of writing comes from seeing the reaction from readers. Did it make you smile or laugh, did it make you cry, hopefully happy tears? Did you fall in love with Flick and Luke as much as I did? I would absolutely love it if you could leave a short review on Amazon. Getting feedback from readers is amazing and it also helps to persuade other readers to pick up one of my books for the first time.

Thank you for reading.

Love Holly x

ALSO BY HOLLY MARTIN

Midnight Village Series

The Midnight Village

Meet Me at Midnight

Apple Hill Bay Series

Sunshine and Secrets at Blackberry Beach

The Cottage on Strawberry Sands

Christmas Wishes at Cranberry Cove

Wishing Wood Series

The Blossom Tree Cottage

The Wisteria Tree Cottage

The Christmas Tree Cottage

Jewel Island Series

Sunrise over Sapphire Bay

Autumn Skies over Ruby Falls

Ice Creams at Emerald Cove
Sunlight over Crystal Sands
Mistletoe at Moonstone Lake

∾

The Happiness Series
The Little Village of Happiness
The Gift of Happiness

∾

The Summer of Chasing Dreams

∾

Sandcastle Bay Series
The Holiday Cottage by the Sea
The Cottage on Sunshine Beach
Coming Home to Maple Cottage

∾

Hope Island Series
Spring at Blueberry Bay
Summer at Buttercup Beach
Christmas at Mistletoe Cove

Juniper Island Series

Christmas Under a Cranberry Sky

A Town Called Christmas

White Cliff Bay Series

Christmas at Lilac Cottage

Snowflakes on Silver Cove

Summer at Rose Island

Standalone Stories

The Secrets of Clover Castle (Previously published as Fairytale Beginnings)

The Guestbook at Willow Cottage

One Hundred Proposals

One Hundred Christmas Proposals

Tied Up With Love

A Home on Bramble Hill (Previously published as Beneath the Moon and Stars

For Young Adults

The Sentinel Series

The Sentinel (Book 1 of the Sentinel Series)

The Prophecies (Book 2 of the Sentinel Series)

The Revenge (Book 3 of the Sentinel Series)

The Reckoning (Book 4 of the Sentinel Series)

STAY IN TOUCH...

To keep up to date with the latest news on my releases, just go to the link below to sign up for a newsletter. You'll also get two FREE short stories, get sneak peeks, booky news and be able to take part in exclusive giveaways. Your email will never be shared with anyone else and you can unsubscribe at any time
https://www.subscribepage.com/hollymartinsignup

Website: https://hollymartin-author.com/
Email: holly@hollymartin-author.com
Facebook: facebook.com/hollymartinauthor
Instagram: instagram.com/hollymartin_author
Twitter/X: x.com/HollyMAuthor

Published by Holly Martin in 2025
Copyright © Holly Martin, 2025

Holly Martin has asserted her right to be identified as the author of this work.
All rights reserved. No part of this publication may be reproduced, stored in any retrieval system, or transmitted, in any form or by any means, electronic, mechanical, photocopying, recording or otherwise, without the prior written permission of the author.
This book is a work of fiction. Names, characters, businesses, organisations, places and events other than those clearly in the public domain, are either the product of the author's imagination or are used fictitiously. Any resemblance to actual persons, living or dead, events all locales is entirely coincidental.

978-1-913616-64-9 paperback
978-1-913616-65-6 Large Print
978-1-913616-66-3 Hardback
978-1-913616-67-0 audio

Cover design by Dee Dee Book Covers